DIVE
BOMBING

I should like to thank especially Jonathan Ashley for his great help and encouragement, James Kinsella, Vitalijus Giedrys and Andy Reynolds for aiding my research; also Luke and Rose Ashley for their support, Paul Ashley for the layout of his Grove Road flat, and Catherine Coe for her insightful editing.

Author's note:

Travonia is an invented country lying between Bulgaria and Romania, whose eastern border is on the Black Sea.

ORCHARD BOOKS
338 Euston Road, London NW1 3BH
Orchard Books Australia
Level 17/207 Kent Street, Sydney, NSW 2000

First published in the UK in 2012 by Orchard Books

ISBN 978 1 40831 392 3

Text © Bernard Ashley 2012

DIVE BOMBING

BERNARD ASHLEY

ORCHARD

OPENER

Charlie was in the audience at Sol Newman's when the car bomb exploded. His mother was on the small stage of the Dover Street jazz club, with Ron Morton at the piano that night. She looked great and she sounded great. Her hair gleamed against her head as she sang Aretha Franklin's 'If You Don't Think', her gospel-voiced lows and highs coming out like rum truffles. It was classic Sally Julien, and Charlie felt that sheen of ice on his skin that always thrilled him when he saw her perform. She was his mum, his dear mum, and she was a star.

She had just got to the line 'I'll stand by your side' when Sol Newman sidled up to her at the microphone and said something behind his cupped hand. She looked startled – Sally Julien wasn't used to being interrupted in the middle of a set, not even by the owner of a club famous for his late-night TV music show. But she listened to him, then shook her head; he nodded, and turning back to the audience she interspersed the words of the song with the warning she'd just been given.

'There's a dodgy motor out the front,
Darling trust my love.

Leave by the kitchens *while the world goes round,*
Happiness an' heartache share the same bed –
Out through that door's where the back way's
 found…'

Some went, but most stayed. A bomb had demolished the front of the Travonian Embassy in Fulham a fortnight before, and MI5's threat level was still at 'critical', but the anti-terrorist squad had made some key arrests of Travonian troublemakers, there wasn't the fear of being in London that there'd been even a week before, and people were getting used to walking past parked cars without the adrenalin squirting.

Sally finished the song and while the audience applauded she had a quick word with Ron Morton at the piano. His head down, he ran his fingers over the introduction to 'Respect', and Sally went back to the microphone with a beautiful smile on her face.

Charlie's dad patted his knee. 'The show goes on, Kid,' Stevie said.

And with a sound like nuclear fission the car bomb exploded outside. Dover Street jigged, the walls shook and shed their paint. A hurricane turned the jazz club inside out. The blast sucked the air and siphoned Charlie's lungs. Deafened, he could only see the screaming.

But Sol Newman's was below ground level. No one down there seemed to be hurt by anything worse than shock and panic, getting out through the kitchens. And that's what they did, Charlie and his mother pulled through by Stevie: Sally screeching out in the rush.

1

Travonia's main airport was in a state of high alert. It was all tension and fear, as if a visa was needed to breathe in and out. The check-in queues were patrolled by armed police in flack jackets and visored helmets, and the predominant sound was not of voices but of hard boots on the tiled floor. Charlie looked around, trying not to move his head. The atmosphere here was so different from the gym at Naraiova University the night before when a rocking audience of students and other fans had whistled and cheered his dad's band, No Rider. Stevie Peat had sung his satirical lyrics in a place filled with fellow feeling, and while the crew did the load-out the chat around the merchandise stall afterwards had been easy, and free. But the airport was definitely a different place to be, like another country.

Charlie and his dad shuffled forward as Flight AF2789 from Naraiova International to London City Airport crept up the departures board.

'What's going on? It wasn't like this when I came.' Charlie had spent four days of the second week of the Easter holiday with No Rider – in the splitter van, sleeping in his dad's hotel rooms, and seeing two concerts

– a short, chancy break to keep him in touch with Stevie.

'Political crap,' his dad said. 'Don't get me going on the state of this country.'

There was a shout from a nearby check-in queue as a man was pulled out of it and thrown to the floor by two policemen, one standing over him with a Kalashnikov aimed at his head.

'Bit harsh for dropping a wrapper.'

But it wasn't funny. The man – who wasn't young – was dragged to his feet and frog-marched towards an unmarked door.

'Give me our own feds,' Charlie said. 'Riot shields instead of rifles.'

'We'll be all right. And you'll be back home in three hours.'

'But you won't.'

Stevie shook his head. 'Don't worry about me. Like Billy Joel's song, "We didn't start the fire". It's their own political crap – and I'm a rocker. We don't leave it to other people to kill us – we usually do that for ourselves.'

Charlie smiled. His dad wasn't one of the spaced-out wild boys, and it was totally impossible he'd ever get that low. Unlike…

His dad must have wished he hadn't just said what he had. 'Don't worry, Kid. Mum's in the best place possible for finding out what's up with her. And that's why I'm out here. I wish like hell I was back home, but that place costs; the best always does, you know that.'

'Sure.' Charlie's mother had been in the Stage Left care home out in Essex for a month of the six weeks since the Dover Street explosion; Dr Leigh was said to be the best psychiatrist in the business.

'Tell her I love her. I'll ring her tonight, but say the tour's going well, no fall-outs yet; and give my best to your nan and grandad.' Not his love, of course. 'Are the Groans treating you OK?' 'The Groans' was Charlie's infant name for grown-ups and it had stuck on his grandparents. 'Not overstuffing you on Hallelujah Pie?'

Charlie hoped his face gave nothing away. 'It's not too bad.' His mum's parents belonged to an ultra-evangelical church.

'Good man. They're meeting you at the airport?'

'Today's St Thomas Sunday, first after Easter...'

'I *doubt* they'll miss that, then!' Stevie gave it a beat. *'Doubt! Thomas!'*

'You can do better than that.' But as well as looking up the church calendar, Charlie had done his London Transport homework. The Groans lived in Leytonstone. 'It's dead easy. London City to Stratford on the DLR, then two stops on the Central line. I'll be OK.'

'Text me.' Stevie put his arm around him and gave him a hug. 'And get yourself into that Bow-bells outfit.'

A lot of talk these four days had been about Charlie getting into the Rubber Girders student rock band.

'Do the Jimi Hendrix dive bomb for 'em, bump 'em up.'

'Wish I could.'

'Work on it. I've shown you – find a harmonic and use your trem bar.'

'It's not so hard on its own – it's finding the harmonic in the middle of a riff.'

'Practice, Kid, practice.'

They were at the front of the check-in queue now, being watched by the largest policeman Charlie had ever seen. The routine questions were put and answered, and he was given his boarding pass.

'You go through, then. I won't hang about – transport call's for eleven, and I need to sort a load of stuff with Vikki.'

Vikki Basescu was the local tour manager. No Rider was Stevie's band, but she was from Travonia and took a lot of the hassle for him.

'We're driving out east to Troilova. Tuesday and Wednesday, two-gig booking.'

'Don't break any strings.'

'Nor you, Kid. I'll see you. And get behind the Hammers. Three matches, one point; we badly need a win.'

'Dream on, Dad.'

'Send me the score.'

'Will do.'

With his rucksack on his back – all Charlie carried, no waiting around at baggage carousels – he rubbed cheeks with his dad and walked through the departures door past a line of dead-eyed police. He didn't look back. He and his dad never did when they went their separate ways, unlike Charlie and his mother, who always competed with each other to give the last wave.

The dirty white van was so nondescript that a traffic warden would have to check the expiry date on its licence. At first glance the man at its rear doors seemed like someone's old uncle. His skin was yellowish, his eyes a watery blue, and wispy white hair poked out from under a woollen hat that stuck up like the archbishop's mitre he wore in religious services. But his stare could stop his compatriots' hearts. Zanko Boev was overseeing the loading of the van by two others who were carrying laptops, holdalls, and bin liners across the pavement of Bath Street, off the Tottenham High Road. The premises they were leaving was a rented shop, its plate-glass window lined on the inside with old newspapers. One of the other men – fat, with a snagged jumper – was making hard work of the carrying; while the third, as spare as a willow cane and with a mouth like twin blades on a razor, did two journeys to his one.

The van doors were closed. The fat man went to the front, but Boev tapped him on the shoulder and said, 'Double-check! We've lost enough.' The man obeyed him immediately, and Boev sat in the passenger seat while the others returned to the shop to look in empty cupboards and under the stairs.

'Nothing.' The man with the razor mouth got into the driving seat, while the fat man pulled himself into the back like a pregnant seal over rocks. But before he could twist his body to sit, the van was driving off, and he was rolling about in the removals.

Charlie's Air France flight came into London City Airport in a steep 5.5° descent. He saw the Thames and Tower Hamlets as the ground rushed up to meet him, and he gave the pilot nine out of ten for putting the Avro down so smoothly.

Without having to wait for baggage Charlie was quickly onto the DLR; but not to Stratford, as he'd told his dad. Instead, he changed at Canning Town and headed on the tube to Mile End, where he came up into the street and stopped to text as promised: The eagle has landed.

He thanked God that even the latest BlackBerry wouldn't give away his location: because instead of being at the Groans' place in Leytonstone he was heading home – to his real home, the Peats' own place, the family flat in Grove Road. This was where he lived, where he belonged, where he longed to be living again with his dad and with his mum – her back to being Sally Julien again. Apart from him checking the post once a week, the flat was supposed to be shut up while his dad was away on the No Rider tour of Eastern Europe. But it wasn't. It was being lived in – by him.

'Mile End Towers', as his dad called it, was in a modern development of four-storey buildings, with its own front door up a flight of steps from the street. Their flat consisted of the ground floor and the basement, which opened out at the back onto a patio; and beyond that was their private parking space.

It was ideal for Stevie, and for Sally when she was home, a hundred metres from the tube and across the road from a breath of air in Mile End Park. The area was mega-busy with students from Queen Mary College

– a cosmopolitan corner where no one would look twice at a black soul singer, or a famous white lead guitarist whose band sometimes played on Jools Holland's or Sol Newman's TV shows. And the flat was ideal for Charlie's secret life. Tall even for sixteen, he could come and go like a second-year undergrad without anyone taking any notice. To keep himself as private as possible – no stupid slip-ups or expected updates – he had cut himself off from any Facebook stuff, riding Bijan's and Francine's jibes at college, who couldn't believe the Groans could have the power to bar him from social networking. But his life was enough of a tangle of lies without making up stuff about all his ins and outs, so he'd shut himself down until his mum was better. Like anyone on a desperate secret mission, Charlie Peat had to be a different person to different people, especially since that mission was all about the person he loved most in the world.

He let himself into the flat, stepped over days of postal trash, and tapped Bridget's number into his mobile. Bridget – a nurse at Stage Left – was his first line of contact with his mother, to keep him briefed.

The Irish voice didn't sound miffed that this was half-past ten on a Sunday night. 'You're back, are you – or stuck in some godforsaken airport?'

'I'm back.'

'An' how's your da?'

'He's fine. But how's my mum?' Charlie held his breath for the reply. It was her state of health that was driving him these days, her getting back to being the person she'd been before that bastard bomb – and from the second he'd got on that flight out to Travonia he'd kicked himself for taking those days out from seeing her. But he'd told himself he was doing his duty by his dad, giving him fuller reports on how she was than he got on the phone; and didn't fathers need family contact, too? But these days he lived for how his mother was doing. Now a huge feeling of guilt sat inside him like an indigestible meal – after all, wasn't he living in the flat on his own so that he could get to see her as often as he could? Taking time out in Travonia had definitely been chancy.

'Oh, she's all right. Not too bad, shall we say? Be the delighted biddy for seein' you, that's for sure.'

'Give her my love in the morning.' Patients like his mother were allowed their own phones at certain times only; according to Dr Leigh, too much outside contact wouldn't help while she was in her current stage of treatment. 'It's the first day of the summer term tomorrow, only a half day at college. Tell her I'll be out in the afternoon.'

'Our girl will be sitting up ready.'

'Cheers, Bridget.'

'Give her love to the ol' Ma an' Pa.'

'I will,' Charlie promised. Or, would, if they weren't five miles away.

He stood in the living room and took stock. Right or wrong for going, he was back now from seeing his dad, who was playing and singing better than ever: composing, too – with an edgy lead song on the new album, 'Spittle Pavement'. And that was what No Rider was all about, gritty lyrics with thumping good music. The band was earning good money with a great student following on this Eastern European tour. If it hadn't been for the police at the airport, Charlie would have felt solid about all that side of things. He and his dad had talked about it in Travonia, and they both knew why he had to be out there.

'I want to be back home holding her hand, Kid. But I've got to be here. It's this old rocker's earnings that give her the best shot at getting better.'

DMA Promotions fixed up plenty of international tours for No Rider because east European promoters paid top money to British bands that did Stevie's sort of mocking rock, singing their spiky stuff in English to people who daren't voice it themselves. What he'd said at the airport was right – Charlie's mother was definitely in the best place, and that best and expensive place could only be paid for by work like the Travonia tour, especially its big whopping-fee finale. If No Rider weren't doing what they did, Sally Julien would soon be in an overcrowded NHS ward – instead of a four-star care home, with a top psychiatrist on her case.

'I can phone her and send stuff, but it's you who's got to be there for me, Kid.'

'I know. I am. I try to be.'

'Good man.'

Bugger! Big downer! *'Not too bad!'* Bridget's caginess told him his mum wasn't marvellous, probably gone backwards with him not going out there this end of the week – although he'd see her tomorrow, and he could judge for himself. At least the Groans hadn't been at the airport waiting for him with a police escort, so they hadn't got suspicious – yet. And the same as always, they hadn't been in touch with Stevie. He'd never been their sort; they even shook their heads at taking money for their grandson's food and keep. Right now, though, to keep himself free to go on visiting his mother, he'd got to look normal to everyone else; so boxes for him to tick were clothes for the morning and remembering his debit card for buying school meals. Then tomorrow he could get to see his mother in the afternoon, and hopefully sort out the date of his audition for Rubber Girders. Francine would know when that was. All of which boiled down tonight to an Air France baguette, looking out a shirt, and a quick practice to get the feel of his own guitar – but keeping the sound down. The last thing he wanted was Miss Portland from next door poking her nose in. If that woman thought he was living here on his own she'd have to do her duty – and if Social Services sent him back to the Groans that would be gross.

He took a half-filled bottle of flat Coke from the fridge and drank it standing up between bites of the baguette. Suddenly, in an angry grenade of a chuck, he sent the plastic hurtling at the back door. Those bastard bombers! It shouldn't be like this tonight. He should be down here boiling rice while his mother stirred her special Sunday night Mustique curry, singing along with one of her spirituals. And they'd be raising their glasses to his dad out in Travonia, and going over their week to come: an audition for him and a gig for her. Instead of which, here he was on his own, living this lie just so he could get to see her when he wanted. And it was crucial he should do that – or any chance of her getting back to being Sally Julien would go further and further away. He was her best hope. It was everything he was here for.

He threw the baguette into the bin – and chased the plastic bottle around the kitchen, stamping, stamping, stamping on it until it was split and flattened. And instead of the words of a spiritual, he swore, and swore; at the end of which he still didn't feel any better. He never should have gone away.

Zanko Boev was organising the new safe house. It was in a terrace waiting to be pulled down as part of the Tottenham re-development following the riots of 2011. It was a good place to hide: the people in this street were the sort who came and went without ever knowing a neighbour.

Boev's large fingers fixed a religious icon on the wall of the small front room. In agonised detail it showed Christ on the Cross, picked out against a flaking gold-leaf background. Boev stepped back to check that it was straight, and after making a small adjustment he bowed deeply to it. A line of painted saints stood along the mantelpiece, and draped over the backs of the armchairs were heavy embroideries of religious scenes. With its candlesticks and hassocks and the smell of incense, the room could have been three hundred years old.

The front room upstairs was twenty-first century. Rajov Tomescu, the man who'd been thrown about in the back of the van, was master of his own space now, setting up the communications centre. Two laptops, a short-wave radio, and a neat collection of phones and GPS equipment were set out along a trestle table, and with dainty fingers he was making contact with someone a long way off in Eastern Europe.

Down in the kitchen at the back of the house, Otto Stoica – a man with explosives under his fingernails – was making green bean soup, adding chicken, parsley and dill, stirring with forensic precision.

A handbell rung by Zanko Boev took both men into the holy room. They each nodded twice; once to Christ on the Cross and once to their leader. All three remained standing.

'We've had two men captured by carelessness, who are taking responsibility for the car bombs. But we have to stay free,' Boev said, wheezing in a voice that would never be disobeyed. 'So, the rules.' He stared at Stoica. 'You don't leave in daylight: shops around here are open very late. You don't stand with your back to the shop door. You don't go direct, and you don't come back direct. You check often, you stop, you double and loop – even going to the grocer, and especially to the electric or hardware store.'

Stoica nodded. He knew all this, of course.

'And you don't stay "live" long enough for a fix,' he told Tomescu. 'They tracked us to the last place. Remes reports they arrived at the shop just fifteen minutes after we'd gone. But they don't know where we are now – and it has to stay like that until after the victory.'

Stoica and Tomescu nodded again at what he had said.

'So now we pray.'

They all kneeled, Stoica helping Boev his archbishop down. Boev led them in reciting an Exhortation of the Eastern Orthodox Church beginning 'Beloved in the Lord'; but at the end of it, after the Amen, they added in defiant voices, 'May the means of the return of Mother Church to our sinful country be forgiven.'

And the eyes in each face showed how up for killing they were, to get what they wanted.

2

Charlie's trip out to Debden to see his mother was dead easy; it was Central line all the way. But his visit to the care home wasn't going to be an easy one; after missing seeing her for those four days, and from Bridget's *'Not too bad'* the night before, he knew she'd have gone backwards. The Groans at Leytonstone could never know how different she was when he went instead of them, which thank God wasn't very often. They just didn't get on, and they knew they left her worse than when they went. But he was everything to her, he and his mother had always been a pair; they seemed to know what the other was thinking, and liked the same things. He made her laugh, and she made sure her gigs never stopped her being his mum. At the end of every visit she was more the old Sally Julien again, and he was rock-solid certain he was crucial to her getting better, the way blood and bone-marrow matches are crucial to a transplant. Sadly, the Groans didn't go along with the care home stuff at all. They thought she should be trusting God to get her out of the mess she was in; and they sincerely believed they were doing their best for Charlie by stopping him from seeing her too often. They would visit her now and then, but he was their new hope, and had to be spared the upset of seeing her too much at Stage Left. *'You've got a good brain, Charles, and you owe it to Jesus and yourself to do well at college. Nothing's got to upset your mind and take you away from your books.'* This was why he'd had to stop living with them, why he'd told them the lie that Stevie had left the Travonia tour to come home to London. He'd had to free himself up for what was a million times more important to him than any AS grades could ever be.

That morning at college had been difficult. It had reminded Charlie of what life was like before the bomb – but how that was all in the past. Back in the sixth-form room it had been like playing a part. Luckily, Bijan Shafei didn't always 'read' other people. He was obsessed with two things: football and strike aircraft – he was determined to be a fighter pilot – and after he'd gone off about a shouting match between two West Ham players in a mid-week fixture: 'All we needed – two back-four players colliding mid-air and having a verbal dog-fight', he was back onto military aircraft. Today his new find had been the operational name given to the Russian MiG-23, the Flogger. 'I bet that can whip across the sky!' And, no surprise, either: the word 'striker' always had a double meaning for old Bijan.

And then Charlie had seen Francine, who was keyboard player in the Rubber Girders – which he kept telling himself was not the reason he wanted to get into the band. Blonde hair with a geometric cut, flashing eyes, and the smile of an angel? No way – it was the music, wasn't it, *the music*, not the nights out on gigs together.

Oh, yes.

These past couple of weeks he'd tried harder to keep normal with her, but she'd seen a difference in him, even asking him why he'd put a plate-glass window between them. Today, though, she'd been excited again, telling him the Rubber Girders' audition was the next night, Tuesday.

Shit! Tomorrow night? And him just back from four days away from his mother...

'Well, it's not really an audition, Charlie. They said you can sit in and they'll listen to you.' Followed by what Charlie got told a lot. 'But you needn't think being Stevie Peat's son's going to cut any ice.'

'As if!' he'd said. 'As if!'

'Just make it, that's all. And do your stuff...'

'Sure.'

And then Francine had made a face that asked, 'Is anything getting through to you?'

It had been a totally difficult morning.

Before the Central line tube rattled up out of its tunnel Charlie made a last check on his reflection. He'd got a lot of ground to make up, so he wanted to look good for his mum. His dark hair had a slight curl to it, and his eyes were brighter than they deserved to be after all those No Rider late nights. Looking into the train window he reckoned he was a decent mix of Stevie Peat and Sally Julien; and he knew she'd like the shirt he'd chosen, showing up his golden skin. To Stevie he was 'Kid', to his mum he was 'Prince' – her Prince – and he needed everything going his way to help her beat her demons.

Charlie was short-breathed with nerves as he took the bus from Debden station to within a ten-minute walk of the gates of Stage Left. This was the five-star care home for performers who fell ill, or got old. It was in an old country house, long, and plastered white, with stables and outhouses stretching out at the back. Charlie had seen it with his dad before his mother had come here. The main building had a kitchen, a dining room, a lounge, and a conservatory that could all have been in a posh hotel; upstairs, large rooms had been split into small individual units. And in one of these, overlooking the gardens, was his mother, the soul singer Sally Julien, temporarily 'not available for bookings' thanks to that diabolical terrorist attack.

Charlie spoke his name into the entry phone and pushed the gate. He gave his name again at the door of the house, and he signed in at reception.

'How's she doing?' he asked Vera, who was behind the desk in the hall.

But Vera could never be drawn on anything. Stevie reckoned she had probably been a theatrical agency receptionist, who smiled at everyone but would never say anything about auditions, gigs or tours. Madam Vera Clamp-mouth.

'I haven't seen her today, Charlie. No adverse reports that I've heard. But go up.' So she knew enough to tell him that.

'Is Bridget on duty?'

'I haven't seen her, lovie.'

Of course she hadn't. Charlie walked up the creaky staircase and went along the corridor to his mother's room. Along the walls were pictures of stage and concert greats – with their names underneath for anyone who didn't know them: Laurence Olivier, Cleo Laine, Joan

Sutherland, Peggy Ashcroft, Ronnie Scott, Shirley Bassey. He walked past a couple of open doors where people were reading, or listening through headphones, until he came to his mother's room. There was a star on every door, and beneath his mother's was a slotted-in card with her name on it.

He knocked, and went in. His mother was sitting with her back to the window, the afternoon sun behind her. Her hair was combed out, making it seem as if he was seeing her through gauze; not solid, almost a ghost.

'Hiya, Mum.'

She said nothing. He guessed she was staring at him, but in the glare he couldn't be sure.

'How're you doing?' He came into the room and took the quickest of looks around the walls for some clue. Was anything new – a different show card or album cover to show she'd been thinking about life before the bomb? But the pictures on her noticeboard hadn't been changed, and the TV/audio centre was switched off, as usual. The door to the en-suite shower room was shut, the poster on it the same as before – Sally's last big one at the Brixton Academy: she'd done headline gigs in a few iconic places before the terrorist attack.

He kissed her. She didn't move. He gave her the box of chocolates he'd bought at Mile End, which she let slip to the floor. He left it there, sat on the bed and started talking.

'Dad sends his love, and the Groans. The tour's doing well, all the venues sold out. And I've got No Rider's new album, I'll play it before I go.'

She didn't reply. This hadn't been unusual when she'd first come here, but it was steps back from his last visit when she'd asked what support bands were on Stevie's tour. She'd definitely lost ground. It was going to be uphill again – and, God! was he sorry he'd let her down.

'Had a good practice last night on the old Tanglewood.' He laughed. 'But I still can't do the dive bomb.'

Nothing.

'Flights were good. Air France does for me over easyJet every time. They fly you through a better class of cloud.'

Still nothing.

'I killed next door's cat and skinned it for dinner. Lovely.'

Not even a disgusted look. In the old days she'd have come back with something about it not being as good as chilli con canary.

He thought about saying something really shocking, but he knew shock tactics weren't the way through

– it was shock that had brought her here, wasn't it? According to Bridget, Dr Leigh was talking about 'selective amnesia': subconsciously choosing not to remember some particular bad memory.

'But she knows about the bombing...'

'Something else, Charlie. Something that was part of it...'

And Charlie knew how his mum would sometimes smack the side of her head as if she was trying to force her brain to sort itself out, trying to get at something to do with that bomb blast – a hole in the memory that might have been just the ticket if it hadn't stopped her being the Sally Julien he wanted back.

Asking that question about support bands last week had been a peak; but Charlie knew he wasn't going to get any glimpse of the old Mum this time. He stroked her hand and a quick thought shot into his brain of when it would have been her hand stroking his. Whatever it took, he would never leave her for more than a day again – he was more determined than ever not to be sent back to the Groans. He let the room fall quiet. The sound of mowing came through the window, a horse snorted somewhere, and downstairs a piano was being played. And now he heard her sobbing. She still hadn't moved, but her fingers were working a tissue to dust and tears were running down her cheeks. He dried them, put his arm around her and kissed her again; then bent to pick up the chocolates to show them to her.

'No good,' she said, way down in her throat.

'What's no good, Mum?' She *mustn't* give up; giving up would be the worst thing ever.

He had to wait a long time.

'What's no good?'

She coughed, drily. 'Milk chocolate. Dairy's no good for the voice.'

'Ah. Sorry. I'll remember that.'

Feeling crap, he reckoned that was about as far as he was going to get that afternoon, but he slid No Rider's new album into the system and played her the start of it, Stevie's 'take' against right-wing liberals.

'Spittle on the pavement
But you stooped for twenty pence;
Put-downs and promises you treated just the same.
You took the middle of the road or you sat upon the fence
And you never knew the difference when it came.'

But she didn't react. She sat still and stared ahead with a look on her face that said she expected nothing from anything or anyone, not even from him or her Stevie.

He switched off the machine and left the album for her. When he kissed her goodbye she murmured, 'Thank you.' But for what? he wondered. For zilch? For not deserting her for ever and coming back to see her?

'See you soon,' he said and she nodded, ever so slightly.

And that was the best he was going to get, for today.

That night at the Brixton Academy had been what it was all about. Stevie was away on tour and so Charlie went with her as her main man. She was in dressing room number one, nearest to the stage, with its own shower and lavatory. Ron Moreton was in the number two, and the Stan Pearl trio, who did the first half and backed in Sally's set, were in the number three. Down in the dressing-room corridor it was all high-fives, catching up, running order, and then came the sound checks, with Charlie as much a part of it as anyone, his mum's unofficial tour manager for the night.

And she was great. She always was, of course, but that night was special. OK, she hadn't filled the venue – the Brixton Academy is big in the 'large hall' league – but it was over three-quarters full, and everyone was there for her. She did her set, and then her encores, and they wouldn't let her off without her reprising a couple more. And finally she took everyone by surprise.

Instead of getting offstage on a 'high', she brought it all down with a follow-spot closing in on her face, singing 'The Man That Got Away' – *The night is bitter, the stars have lost their glitter* – shading her voice down as the light faded, and walking out of the spot and off stage-right. Not to come back. It was magic. Charlie was waiting in the wings with a towel and, throwing his arms around her, he protected her down to the dressing room and took her inside, shutting the door – where they stood hugging each other until she stopped shaking.

'Fantastic, Mum!'

This was Sally Julien. This was Sally Julien, and Charlie Peat, her 'Prince'.

And this was what he was going to bring back. Him and her, together.

The transport choice for the No Rider tour had been between sleeper bus, or splitter van and hotels. Stevie and Vikki Basescu had gone for a splitter van. Sleeper buses were for kids who didn't mind having no privacy, and who didn't need much sleep; they'd got the name of those vehicles all wrong. No Rider wasn't a rough-edge band of tear-aways; after a gig, drummer Nicky Harris might stay on for the DJ, and keyboard player Deano Rivera might go out clubbing, but the rest were more into a brandy and a read of their messages in the hotel. And Vikki promised that all the hotels they'd be using in Travonia would be of a decent standard, so that was the clincher; en-suite bathrooms, even in a one-star place, meant no queueing at the venues for showers.

After a long drive the band and crew had arrived at Troilova, dropping off at two hotels, band first, crew second, where the van parked. The load-in call for the concert was 9 a.m. next day, and the band could easily walk to the Sala Muzica for the sound check at five.

Some of the band slept in late, but Stevie liked some exercise in the mornings, and Deano Rivera – who nowadays put the notes to Stevie's words – was restless, so they took a walk together around the town.

Troilova, way over in the east of the country, was a third the size of the capital, and the ethnic mix was different. There weren't too many black or Asian faces here, mostly the greyish-white of old marble; cold, and no smiles.

'You sure it's a sell-out tonight?' Deano wanted to know.

'Supposed to be.' Deano was a young replacement for Stevie's old writing partner Denny Drew, who'd died from painkiller abuse; Deano hadn't been to Travonia before. 'Plenty of mavericks, just as unhappy here as they are down south.' No Rider gigs pulled in students, doctors, teachers, lawyers, artists, and some of the old Russian regime's socialist workers. 'People wanting a better society.' Stevie threw a stone into the wide river, not making much of a splash. The pair of them were on the old-order side of the Danube, with beggars sitting against walls and packs of roaming dogs scavenging from the squalor. The other bank of the river was dominated by up-market apartments. 'Travonia is two countries any way you slice it.'

'Can't smell much nightlife around here.'

'Not much life, full stop.' Stevie pulled Deano's arm and turned them towards the centre of the city. Deano wasn't Denny Drew – he sometimes put Stevie in mind of Charlie – but he was a Billy Joel on keyboard and an up-and-coming composer. 'I'll show you the old cathedral with its Soviet bullet holes.'

'Find me a Smirnoff, more like.'

But as they walked the broken pavement their eyes weren't set so much on old wars or vodka as the numbers of No Rider posters on the phone cabinets and tram shelters – the headline band for two nights at the Sala Muzica. And their musicians' body-clocks were set for the sound-check at five, the seven-thirty doors, and the nine o'clock start with Stevie and Denny's rousing opener 'Hold Back the Thames'.

'Mixed-up old country, then,' Deano said.

'But where the touring money is,' Stevie replied. 'Some of these folk go without a lot to come to a No Rider gig.'

'Putting us on which side of the fence?' Deano went walking on.

'Good question, kid! Good question.' And Stevie walked on with him.

And it might have been deliberate, or it might have simply been that his mind was on other things, but Stevie said nothing to Deano about the convoy of three white police vans he'd just seen cruising across on the other side of the square; the sort of vans that had been parked outside the airport on Sunday when Charlie went home.

3

The big threat to him at the Grove Road flat was his next-door neighbour. Maeve Portland had been a journalist until her paper went bust, and she still acted like a spider on its web; the slightest vibration and she wanted to know what caused it. And there was one vibration that worried her a lot. Every autumn when the Peats' central heating started up, sludge in the system would get their boiler rattling through the party wall – but, sited in a cupboard with recording studio insulation inside the door, it wasn't nearly so loud on the Peats' side. Annually, Maevy-baby would come to check that she wasn't about to be blown up. 'We're not going to have an explosion, are we, Mr Peat? I should be very cross if I woke up dead one morning.' She'd threaten to get the flats' caretaker to look at it, but Charlie's dad would say he'd get the engineer in, and the system always righted itself within a couple of days, so it stayed like that from one October to the next. It was the only bum note between the neighbours; put the gas boiler on one side and there was no unfriendliness between them – even Maevy-baby's yearly visit was light and jokey. She had written a great piece about 'Sally Julien – the East

End's Roberta Flack' for the *Guardian*, and she always lit up at the sight of Stevie Peat standing on his front steps. She might be more up for Festival Hall recitals, but she'd also been known to slip across to the O2 for Stevie Wonder or Bruce Springsteen, and she never moaned about Stevie, Sally or Charlie practising.

But she was a real threat to Charlie as he lived his lie. She often put her rubbish in the wheelie-bin just as someone was going out, and as she was going indoors she was usually quite slow at closing her front door. So while Charlie was fooling his dad and the Groans right now, he'd got his work cut out pretending that his mother was living in the flat. When he got close to home he kept tight to the wall like a secret agent in a film, but the last few metres were in open view from all the flats, so it was key ready, run up the steps, no fumbles at the lock, and in through that front door like someone being chased. 'Hi Mum! I'm home,' he'd shout at the party wall. And, of course, his mother was never home herself. When she'd gone into Stage Left, Stevie had told Maevy-baby she was touring in Ireland – he didn't want a piece popping up in the press about Sally Julien in some sort of rehab – but when Charlie had come back from living those weeks of hell with the Groans, he'd made sure to tell her she was back. Now whenever he was caught on the doorstep, his mother was always auditioning, or rehearsing, or seeing her agent, and she'd be home later. This way Charlie had been left in peace for the past month, helped by their neighbour going off to Paris to research a book. But now she was home again, and she was definitely the enemy.

And – shit! – here she was, coming towards him.

'Charlie!' She waved at him along the pavement.

He'd thought he was going to make it. The same as always, his mind was on his mother; she was why he was coming back here in the first place. She'd been in a state yesterday, and he'd been in a state today, never on the right page, uptight with his mates, and accused of being surly by Ms History Hilary. All he'd wanted to do after college that night was get indoors, grab a bite, and practice for his Rubber Girders audition – although he hadn't known until now what he was going to do about that: *had there been a realistic hope of getting out to Debden and back again in time?* Part of his mind had been on the face of his watch, and part of it on chords and scales. But here to put the tin lid on everything was Maevy-baby coming home from Mile End tube, tall and thin, her hair swept up out of her searching eyes – and his full attention had got to be on his secret survival.

'Hi, Miss P.'

Their front steps and doors were next to one another, and, worse luck, instead of stopping at hers, she came on past it, reaching into her messenger bag. But she brought nothing out. 'No, I won't give it to you. It's only a piece about Billie Holiday. I'll give it to Sally when I see her.'

'I'll tell her to give you a knock. If she's in. I think she said something about leaving me a pizza in the fridge, so…'

'It'll keep.'

'Hope so. I fancy beans on toast.' That was the best he could do, try for a laugh.

'Whenever,' she said, and went up her steps.

Charlie let himself into his flat, his shirt in a twist. Maevy-baby knew all about No Rider being away on tour, they'd talked about it, she always said she was proud to be living next door to Stevie Peat the singer-songwriter; so she knew it was just his mother there with him. And at some stage a clever old bird like her would wonder how come she never got a glimpse of Sally Julien, even though she was supposed to have finished her Irish tour. If Maevy-baby had been a crime writer she'd be thinking there was a stiff under the patio. Charlie shook off that cold thought and went down the stairs to the kitchen, where it actually *was* going to be Heinz on toast.

He lived on a baked-beans budget. With his mother

in the care home, and believing that he was with the Groans, Charlie's dad had given him the debit card for 'this and that'. It helped a lot because, with the Groans not asking for money for Charlie's keep, his dad had no idea he was living here like a student at the uni – and the card meant he could still eat. His official weekly job was to come to the flat to check for mail and bills, to send music-business correspondence on to his parents' agent Bernie Jacobs, and to deal with anything else using the card, after talking to his granddad. Stage Left and the big stuff was all direct debit, so the card was for guitar strings, Oyster cards, anything Charlie needed for school, and for emergency repairs to a window or a door lock; but mostly what came out of the hole in the wall was for bread and baked beans – and baked beans, and baked beans.

He ate them cold tonight, feeling even more all-over-the-place than before. He tried to kid himself it was because of next door – but he knew it was something else – a feeling of guilt for even thinking about Charlie Peat for five minutes. With his mother the way she was, he really needed to go to Debden tonight; but all day he'd nursed a wild hope that with buses on time, no waits at Underground stations, and him running when he usually walked, he could get out there and back in time for the Rubber Girders audition. But a lesson over-ran and the buses home from college were crap, and the time had ticked on until a Debden trip out and back before half-seven became mission impossible. Now his stomach rolled with guilt at even thinking about going to Bow, because he knew what he had to do. The state his mother was in, he'd got to go and see her – that was the whole point of him living like this. And Rubber Girders was one of loads of outfits around. Shit, he could start his own band, the Double Life!

He left the Heinz can in the sink – and his guitar in its case. It was a no-brainer. Francine or not – and she'd be dead upset – Rubber Girders had to go on hold. Instead of thinking about practising for the audition he gave up all hope of getting out to Debden and back to the band practice, and showered to wash his conscience clean of even thinking of himself, coming out knowing that risking Francine's friendship by seeing his mother tonight was a cause for which he would fight to the death.

In the Tottenham house two of the extremist Orthodox Christians were on pay-as-you-go phones to Travonian workers' hostels and homes in Lincolnshire, Norfolk, the Scottish borders, East Lothian and Northumberland, as well as to compatriots in Germany and France. The Neo-Vlach terrorist campaign against the Travonia government had to be funded, so Rajov Tomescu was drumming that need into the heads of the migrant gang bosses. Military hardware and explosives were expensive, and so was keeping the mouth of the main Romanian supplier of ex-Kosovan war stockpiles shut. A good slice of the money for materials and bribes needed to come from these migrant workers, which was why two Travonian ruling-party premises had been bombed in London – to encourage those exiles to pay up to see the return of a Neo-Vlach Christian state in the south of the country – on the back of which other opposition groups could change the north. Boev and Tomescu manned the phones, Stoica was security, and a fourth terrorist – Stefan Remes from his safe-house in Kent – went around the country and across the Channel collecting the money.

Today, Boev himself was on more immediate deadly business. He was making a call to a trailer park on the eastern Travonian outskirts of Troilova, and in a cracked voice and an old nomadic language was telling the leader of the regional Neo-Vlach cell that a Land Rover carrying Semtex 1A had crossed the Suceava mountains and was on its way to a farm thirty kilometres from the town. He gave the farm's coordinates. 'Make that rendezvous, cut random samples and check for the blue flame. This is our first attack in the homeland and it's got to go right. Our man takes a taxi at Manta, which he hijacks – and buries the driver in the forest to the west. You meet him with the Semtex 1A. Park the taxi at the target spot – home towns hurt deepest – and set the timer.' And after giving the leader of the cell the detonation time Boev abruptly ended the call, before calling his compatriots to Christian prayer, everything delivered in the same righteous voice.

The concert on the Tuesday was a stormer. The two-thousand-seat Sala Muzica was full, its nineteenth-century plaster hung with modern speakers, strobe lights and spots. Its stage was raked, sloping from the back wall down to the pit, so drum risers, stage boxes and amps all had to be wedged to keep them level. But the band wore in-ear monitors to hear their individual sounds, so they had no clutter of black amps at their feet. All this was important technically, but the soul of No Rider was the fast beat of the music and the radical stuff they sang. Any puffed-up target was good for pricking. Stevie's motto was, 'Let's up the anti!' – and the band was famous for upping it as far as it would go. To cheers and whoops the band ran on: all black T-shirts, black jeans, black trainers – except Deano Rivera in his white frockcoat and long boots, whose only nod to black was the sunglasses he never took off. From 'Hold Back the Thames' to 'Fervour' they played their seventy-five-minute set and a three-song encore, and made sure they all got round to the merchandising stand before the punters got away. Selling their stuff was top priority once they were off; every T-shirt worn was an advert for the band, and the new 'Spittle Pavement' album had to be pushed. The cover showed the band standing in front of the Houses of Parliament, bowing their heads in sorrow – Stevie Peat, lead guitar and vocals, Sean O'Hara, rhythm guitar, Paul Stoner, bass guitar, Nicky Harris, drums and trumpet, and Deano Rivera, keyboard and vocals.

But when they ran into the foyer the five of them were slowed by what they saw. Through the front doors they could see a line of state police stretched across the street, looking hostile. There had been some of this in the south, but they hadn't seen it this far out east.

'What's all this about?' Sean O'Hara asked. 'It's like Derry in the Troubles.'

'Some sort of politics,' Stevie said. 'After the London bombs the government here's dead scared it's going to kick off in the homeland.'

No one said much for a moment. They all knew how badly Sally had been hurt.

'The police were giving it large like this at the airport. And I saw police vans in the town this morning. They're scared the Neo-Vlachs will kick-start the real dissidents...'

'Hey, we're not caught up in a revolution, are we?' Nicky went on signing a drumstick.

Deano autographed the back of a girl's T-shirt, lingering a bit over the spelling. 'They probably think we *are* the revolution.'

'Can't be, if we're playing their big government concert...'

'To keep hot-heads happy,' Vikki said. 'Safety valve.'

The band went on signing CDs, T-shirts, and bare arms. It had been a great show, but as the audience was funnelled out past the police they felt the prickly reality of being in a police state. They had played in places where they were frisked going in and out of venues, and the further 'right' the country, the more dogs they seemed to have for sniffing around musicians for drugs. And now tonight, when Stevie and the others settled in for a drink at the Tuti Hotel, everyone started looking up at the light fittings for secret-service bugs.

* * *

Sally wasn't in her room when Charlie arrived at Stage Left. She was in the lounge, where an elderly trio in grey bowler hats – 'The Debdenaires' – was playing show hits on keyboard, drums and saxophone. Charlie had forgotten this regular Tuesday thing because Bridget had told him his mother never went to it. He hadn't seen so many residents together like this, and he was surprised how different they all were. Some were obviously at Stage Left because they were retired, but a lot were younger. One man not a lot older than himself looked very ill, all his hair fallen out; and a tall woman with a distressing shake seemed to be trying to keep her body spasms in time with the music. The sad thing was, the ill looked ill, the old looked old, and none of them looked showbiz any more. Charlie reckoned a follow-spot directed around the room would have shone straight through them and cast no shadows.

With Bridget sitting next to her, Sally was in the second row of armchairs, staring straight ahead as if her eyes were focused on the far distance, way through the windows and out over the lawns. Bridget saw him and signalled for him to come over, and gave him her seat. 'Sit yourself by our girl. I'm for a cup o' tea – and I'll talk to you later…' She said it with meaning: she needed to talk to him before he went home.

'Hi, Mum.'

'Hi.' Said very flat.

The trio moved without a key change from 'Over the Rainbow' into 'If I Loved You'. An old woman along from Charlie quavered out the first couple of lines, then forgot the rest, but instead of la-la-la-ing she swore like someone blowing a scene in a rehearsal – just for that moment more like an old pro than an old dear.

'Do they ever play your sort of stuff, Mum?' Charlie asked. But he knew the answer to that. The only 'soul' thing about this trio was the sad souls they were, doing their dusty old concert party stuff to a dead-easy audience.

But his question triggered something; his mother was suddenly very agitated; she rocked in her chair and shook her head wildly, smacking it with her hand as if she was furious with its failure to work.

The old woman along from them had found a few lyrics from somewhere.

Words wouldn't come in an easy way
Round in circles I'd go…'

'What is it?' Charlie took hold of Sally's hand and held it firmly. 'I'm here. Tell me, Mum.'

Suddenly she thrust her face at him, her huge eyes staring into his. 'I did something, Prince! I know I did something. But…I can't find what it was…' She pushed back her chair. 'I can't find what I did!' she shouted at the trio. 'But I did something!'

Bridget was back. 'Come on, darlin'.' With an arm around her waist she led Sally to the door. 'We won't be interruptin' the concert…'

Sally held on to Charlie's hand and allowed herself to be led out, as the trio started playing 'Some Enchanted Evening'.

'Let's get you to your room an' a nice cup of tea.'

Meekly, she allowed herself to be led upstairs.

'We nearly know what it was, don't we, darlin'? It was something in the car bomb. It'll come as the shock wears off. But, "Did something"? Like hell! It was the something those devils did to you, sweetheart, and the trauma of it, the same as in the wars. Bless you, nothing's any fault of your own…'

Together, they made Sally comfortable in her bed, with a cup of tea she didn't drink and a biscuit she didn't eat, although she took a tablet that seemed to calm her. And as if Sally was a child, Bridget told Charlie in front of her what the psychiatrist had said.

'Dr Leigh said to try the sing-song, do something out of your ma's usual routine. She's still going with selective amnesia, which can be a symptom of post-traumatic stress disorder, you know, the old shell shock. It's like your mum's brain lets her remember some bits but there's another bit playing hide-and-seek in there, some other nag that's obsessing our girl.'

'So how's the doctor going to dig it out?'

Bridget shrugged. 'It's a long old job, darlin', unlocking something gone down deep. Day to day it's take the tablets for the sweats and the pounding heart, but this week the doctor's upped the long sessions with her, talkin', talkin', talkin'.'

'Sure.' That was what Charlie's dad was touring for, a psychiatrist's time and skill, because anyone could dish out tablets. Sally Julien was definitely in the right place. If anything was going to get her better it was Harley Street's Dr Leigh, helped by a nurse like Bridget. When he'd met Dr Leigh, Charlie had liked the psychiatrist's no-nonsense style; she didn't wave her hands in the air, she pointed at you, and at herself; told them how she'd stabilise Sally first before beginning the real psychiatric treatment. She made you give straight answers to some probing questions, she got you wanting to do right for *her,* which in the end was all about doing right for her patient.

As his mother gave him the weakest of smiles, Charlie knew how dead right he'd been to give Rubber

Girders a miss tonight – and how he was absolutely, double-cracking entitled to be telling his dad and the Groans all sorts of lies to keep on coming to see her. He was going to be important in all this – someone close like him would stand the best chance of unlocking her padlocked memory, not only by coming here day after day, but through any other stuff he might be able to do too.

He looked at the en-suite shower door. He knew what the poster on it was hiding – a poly-filled repair where someone had once head-butted it. And that's what he felt like doing right now, running at it and giving it a great crack – for those terrorist swine, for his kissing goodbye to Francine's friendship, for feeling so twisted up inside all the time that it churned him like a stomach bug. But what good would that do? None. Sweet zilch. He was doing what was best, and he was going to go on doing it against all else until they got a result. Nowadays it was what his shattered life was all about.

4

Klaus Spanu walked over the footbridge from the southern side and onto the platform of Mantu station, mingling with the commuters coming off the 17.50 train. He was youngish with slicked-back dark hair, and could have been one of them, except for what he was carrying – a brand new spade wrapped in the manufacturer's plastic.

Outside, half a dozen yellow taxis and a line of family cars were waiting to meet the train. Spanu went to the first available cab, next in the taxi-queue after a pale-faced man with a laptop.

'How you off for time?' he asked the driver.

'All night. Whatever. Where to?'

Spanu slid into the back seat. 'Brown Scrof Lodge.' This was a country hotel used in the season by hunting parties shooting wild boar.

The taxi driver made a noise with his tongue like the click of dice. Brown Scrof Lodge was a better earner than a short run to the housing project on the outskirts of the town – it was a thirty-kilometre fare into the forest. Pointedly, he switched on the meter.

'You all right for gas?' Spanu asked.

'Enough. You got business out there? The gardens…?'

Being April it was early season, and the Easter weekend was past. But Spanu just grunted from behind his free newspaper.

The driver put on his sunglasses against the low sun, and was still whistling softly when, half an hour later, they reached the forest and Spanu asked him to stop, saying he'd forgotten to pee at the station. And it was Spanu who was wearing those sunglasses when the taxi arrived at a remote farm near Troilova – with no sign inside of the driver, or of Spanu's spade.

There was no question about it, giving Debden all the time it needed had been dead right; hurrying off last night would have been gross. His mother had been in a poor old state – but on the positive side, something new about the night of the bomb did seem to have been nudged inside her head. This could be vital stuff, and he was totally dedicated to helping to find it. But he'd woken with a guilty feeling of selfishness along with his determination. Rubber Girders. In spite of everything he was still really up for getting into that band – he'd wanted it ever since Francine had told him their rhythm guitar was going off to the Royal Academy of Music. He'd dreamt of taking his mother to hear her Prince play in a rated band, and presenting her with CDs from their merchandising. After all, wouldn't it help to show her the hopeful side of life, all part of getting her feeling more normal and back to rights? And it would be getting himself back, too. Rubber Girders were reviewed in the *NME*, and although he could kid himself there were plenty of good bands around, they were definitely the best – and they did need a new rhythm guitar. Francine said they were in no hurry, the guy wasn't going till September, but Charlie knew from his dad that once the band thought they were onto someone they'd start practising together, to make sure they were going to gel before any big gigs came along. And it's always hard to edge out whoever's sitting in.

But he'd blown it now, hadn't he? And, shit! for that, whatever the reason. And he'd blown it with Francine, too. Like Bijan, she knew all about the bomb and his mother's illness, and about Debden, and his dad being in Travonia; but neither of them knew what he was really up to, living at home on his own – and they didn't know his reasons. Francine couldn't know that the Groans would never have gone to Debden in his place last night, and if he'd been living with them, he couldn't have gone himself. And kid himself however much he wanted, Francine was special.

As Bijan often said, Francine was Charlie's co-pilot, the one who did the navigating while he thought he was on his own trajectory; the whole Rubber Girders thing had been in her hands. But Bijan didn't know the mission Charlie was on, so it was best to smile and go along with him. Today, though, Charlie wished he'd brought Francine into his secret. He should have done it before; a girl like her could have helped to cover his back in loads of ways, and didn't they say a problem shared is a problem halved? So, why hadn't he told her what he was up to? The answer was almost too complicated for him to get hold of himself. All he knew was that it came down to loyalty. If Francine knew about him living alone in the Grove Road flat she'd be too close-in to his family for now, and day-to-day he'd have to share more parts of his mother than he wanted to: how she was doing, what she'd said, what the psychiatrist thought. No, it would somehow be wrong to talk of her private business to anyone until she moved on. Sally Julien was a performer who was going to make a come-back. She was just off the scene for a bit, the way performers often are. So Francine and Bijan had been entrusted with knowing she was ill and where she was, and about his concern for her; but until she was a lot better, he only had one main girl – and that was his mother.

All the same, Francine knowing more would have helped him today; helped him a lot. His gut was as twisted as ever when he saw her in the form room, not helped when she gave him a stranger's 'please yourself' look, like someone not caring that you didn't take a freebie off their charity stall. He had texted her on the way out to Debden, but now he'd got to bite the bullet; he did owe her a face-to-face apology. He signalled 'Hi' with a waggle of his fingers. She looked more beautiful than ever today: her blonde hair, those big brown eyes, and teeth that gleamed when she smiled. But she wasn't smiling now.

He went over to her. 'I'm sorry, France…'

She shrugged again, shoulders higher this time.

'I told you why…'

'You did. And I'm totally sorry about your mother. But—'

'Yeah, I know.'

'If it had been a gig last night, what then?'

Charlie nodded. 'Except, it wasn't a gig, and Mum's really not well. Me going away last week, it's pushed her backwards. Soon as I can get her back to where she was, I'm up for everything.'

Francine smiled, just a small one, and put a hand on his arm. 'I did say all that to the band, sort of.'

'Cheers.' *He could have shared more stuff, couldn't he?*

'But don't think you can walk into Rubber Girders anytime just because you're Stevie Peat's son.'

'You said that, and I don't. And the reason I didn't come, was that I'm Sally Julien's son, too.' It came out more saintly than he'd have liked.

'Understood. But come on Friday – and don't miss.'

Today was Wednesday, he'd go to Debden tonight, and again on Thursday, and on Saturday. 'I'll be there, France. Promise.' His gut twisted gastric again. He'd said *promise* and he meant it right now – but he knew darned well that if he had to he'd break it like that.

Oh, God, what would it be like to be normal again, not to have this feeling that a bomb was going to blast open the form-room door any moment?

'Or else, you know…?'

'Definite.'

Bijan came into the form room – short hair and wearing a shirt with epaulettes: after university he was set on flying for the RAF, or the 'Punjabi boys'. 'How'd it go, Hendrix? You set for the O2?'

'Nope. I went out to see Mum.'

'Ah.' Bijan smacked Charlie on the back. He was a good mate, didn't have to be told any more than that.

'But you're coming to the ground to get testimonial tickets, Saturday? Roy Seboa – legend. Personal sales, nine o'clock…'

'Dead right I am.' Charlie couldn't see his mother in the mornings on any day of the week; mornings were when the sessions and treatments were done; but with the Hammers playing away at Arsenal that Saturday, he'd go to Debden in the afternoon.

Bijan pulled out his history folder. 'You ready for this: Charles Stuart's trial and execution?'

'Natch.'

'Up the Commonwealth!'

'Every time.'

'Wish they'd gone for a modern module – the Cold War. MiG Floggers and U-2 spy planes. More up my runway than muskets, pikes and axes.' He slapped his folder. 'Come on, chop chop.' And Bijan was already heading off to the first period of the day.

Charlie rolled his eyes at Francine and followed his friend, gnarled up and sad, wondering when his own life would be that bright and breezy again.

'Home Secretary, could I speak with you a moment?' Erik Bergovic, the Travonian ambassador to the UK, was in the atrium of parliament's Portcullis House where the prime minister was hosting a reception for London's diplomats.

'Certainly, Erik.' The Right Honourable Jo Baker was good at balancing a drink with diplomatic protocol. Not all Home Office business was done at the ministry in Marsham Street, where press cameras flashed whenever foreign diplomats' cars drove in. 'How are you? Are our boys and girls in blue looking after your embassy a bit better?'

'Yes, thank you, madam. But it is on that subject…'

Jo Baker took Bergovic's arm and steered him away from the throng, nearer to the security doors facing the Thames. 'Fire away.'

'You have arrested two of the Neo-Vlach bombers. But I wish you had not.'

The home secretary looked surprised.

'We would get more out of them than your MI5 is permitted.'

'Oi-oi!' She laughed.

'We know the bombs in London were to inspire the Travonian workers here. It's the southern rural class who are in your fields – and it's they who help provide funds for the Neo-Vlach campaign.'

'Yes, we'd come up with something like that, too.'

'But we are picking up more phone chatter at

home, in Travonia. They're planning something in our country, and we believe it's being organised from here, in London.' The smallish bald ambassador twisted his head like a conspirator himself, checking on the closeness of others. 'Zanko Boev. He's most dangerous, and he's leading the insurrection against President Ardeleanu and the Capitalist Freedom Government. We can't pin it on him, but we know Boev planted the London bombs, and we know he's talking in code to cells in Travonia.' He looked seriously into the home secretary's eyes. 'Find Boev, and we will stop all these atrocities.'

Jo Baker gave him a politician's look: a nod of concern followed by a cock of the head that asked, 'What's in it for us?'

'We're opening markets with the Chinese, on special terms. We're doing a deal with the Chinese for the mining of Black Sea minerals, on condition our country stays stable. And we would like to share these special terms with some of our special friends, like Britain, of course.'

'So I'm told by the Department of Trade and Industry.'

'But Beijing will be frightened off by any serious sign of instability. If the Neo-Vlachs make waves—'

'If they muddy the Black Sea, so to speak...'

'—Our special friends cannot benefit.'

The home secretary took a look around the atrium herself. A young man was carrying a footstall through the hall, on which the PM would shortly stand for his speech.

'I'll step up our surveillance. Get our spooks further onboard with all their electronic wizardry.' For a second it looked as if she might reach up to pat the ambassador's shiny head. 'Pull out all the stops to catch the big fish, to mix a metaphor.'

'Thank you, Home Secretary.'

'No problem, Ambassador.'

And they each turned as if to listen to what the PM would say. But the home secretary was already briefing her parliamentary aide. 'For God's sake find that religious crook, Boev. He's not going to make monkeys out of MI5 on my watch.'

'Yes, Minister.'

She squeezed his arm, hard enough to hurt. 'No terrorist scum's skulking in a safe house here – even if the man he wants to bring down *is* a jumped-up little toad.'

Essex was sunny and warm, a bright spring evening as Charlie got off the tube. It put melancholy thoughts in his head of the summer ahead, and cricket in Victoria Park; because all that would be normal, wouldn't it? And as the sun began to dip he thought of the special sunsets he'd shared with his mum, the two of them just looking at them and not feeling the need to speak.

Tonight Sally was in a corner of the grounds that could have been deep in the countryside – if it weren't for the high perimeter wall that could just be seen through the trees. She was wrapped in a bright shawl and sitting on a bench with Bridget. A red ribbon was tying up her hair, and she was talking fast, holding her head a bit higher than she had the night before. To Charlie it was like a photo shot of the old days, when she was planning a tour, or talking about a musical arrangement with Ron Moreton. Bridget was holding her hands, and smiling.

Charlie walked up to them, ready for a smile from his mother; but she just nodded at him.

Bridget shook her head – sort of saying, *Not to worry*. 'Look, darlin', here's a lovely thing, don't you think? Here's your Prince! Here's Charlie, come to see you.' She got up and sat Charlie next to Sally. She clasped her hands in front of her. 'She's in a talking mood today, and on the up side, for sure. Aren't you, sweetheart?' She nodded at Charlie. 'She's had a real long session with Dr Leigh and, guess what?'

Charlie put on a 'can't guess' face, smiling it at his mother.

'She's stopped one of her tablets, hasn't she? The one that did the damping down...'

'Great!'

'The doctor's on the next stage of reducing the medication, and doing more of the...' Bridget searched for the word, like someone who's only delaying so the answer carries more weight. '...Of the *therapy*.'

'Ah.' Charlie took over holding his mother's hands. 'How d'you feel, Mum?'

She stared into his face, then, as if she was making a deliberate decision to do it, she leant forward and kissed him on the forehead.

'I brought you some fruit jellies. Won't harm your voice.' Charlie took the box from his pocket and gave it to her. She put it on the bench. She *was* different today, from the way she'd been last night, but from the old days, too. She'd kissed him, but Charlie felt as if he didn't know her any more, and he didn't know where to go from here. It was like the panic feeling he'd had in the middle of the traffic at a busy crossroads in Naraiova – on his own with stuff flying at him from all the wrong directions.

Bridget looked back towards the house, 'Now you

two have a nice ol' talk. An' when you're finished I'll be waiting with a lovely cup of tea inside.'

She went, and Charlie put his arm around his mother. 'Everyone sends their love. Dad's doing great on the tour; misses you, but it's going great guns. Did he phone?'

She nodded.

'And Nan and Grandad are OK...'

She turned her head to face him, a fast twist. 'And that man?'

This was new. 'What man, Mum? Dad's great, I've told you; so's Grandad...'

'The other man.' She sounded anxious, and impatient, as if Charlie was deliberately not understanding. 'That other man.' She clicked her fingers, as if it was just the name that was escaping her – but at least she hadn't smacked her head.

'What other man? Honest, Mum – I can't think of another man.' What was this? Was she rambling? Had the tablet Dr Leigh stopped been controlling this? Was she mixing real life up with her music – like 'The Man That Got Away' – because she couldn't have a boyfriend, could she? Cheating on his dad was totally out of the question. Charlie would have known. They were all too close for him *not* to know – although the way she sang her songs, the deep meaning she put into them, he'd always had his mother rated as a great actress. So *could* there be someone he and his dad didn't know about? Or *did* Stevie know? Had the psychiatrist's digging turned up some guilty secret? Charlie shook his head. That was so off the radar it wasn't worth brain time.

She lifted her face into the last of the low, red, sun. With light make-up on, she could have been on stage about to sing the blues.

'I don't know any other man – but this here guy loves you, Mum.' He couldn't think of anything else to say.

She smiled at him, a sort of acceptance, for now.

She took her hands out from under his, patted his arm, and gave him back the fruit jellies. 'Nothing to get your teeth into with these,' she said.

But he'd got something to chew on – more than a kid like him could want. What man could she be thinking of? Was someone blackmailing her, did she have a stalker she'd never let on about? And dare he ask his dad what man could be in her head? Was her illness really all about that bomb – or had it triggered something from the past that was lying deep down inside her? Had she got a guilty secret, some person her home and musical life had been keeping hidden, even from her?

Walking back to his bus he kept shaking his own

5

Travonia's president, Gheorghe Ardeleanu, former postman and small-time dealer, always played his 'son of Troilova' card with his hand on his heart – so it was outside the offices of the governing party in Troilova's main square that Klaus Spanu parked the hijacked Manta taxi with two suitcases of primed Semtex 1A explosive in the boot – to blow the heart out of the president's home town.

Cars and vans could park anywhere they wanted in Travonia, across pavements and in front of steps and doors. Taxis sat waiting through change after change at traffic lights, and a lorry leading a line of traffic along a street would just stop, ignoring the congestion it caused. So no one took the slightest notice of the taxi sitting outside the double doors of the CFP office; and in the customary hooting and screeching of the traffic in the town, no one could possibly have heard the ticking detonator, set for ten the next morning when the office would be busy.

Tossing the driver's sunglasses onto the front seat, Spanu wiped his hands down his jeans and headed for Troilova railway station, sending a pre-coded message to London with one click of his mobile phone.

*　*　*

Stevie and the rest of the No Rider band were checking out of their Troilova hotel as the splitter van pulled up with the crew. The load-out from the Sala Muzica had been done the night before under sound engineer Winston Beckford; Kris, the driver, had had a good night's sleep, and everything was set for the drive to Dacai and its university campus – another sell-out two-night stand, Friday and Saturday.

Travonia was a big country – the drive would be more London to Lyons than London to Liverpool – but the Mercedes van was as comfortable as anything on the road. The seats were leather, four around a table with two singles, and three places up front for the driver and two of the crew. It had a plasma TV, a bag of Blu-rays and a stereo sound system; behind the bulkhead at the rear was six cubic metres of space for the gear.

That night there would be the one hotel stop en route, at a small town in a mining area; meanwhile, they could relax, talk when something needed saying, listen to music, snooze, and look at the scenery. They'd driven this road before. Heading south-west away from the mountains, Stevie knew the countryside would be flat and boring: fields of rapeseed, wide strips of this and that, and tightly herded sheep. The tour wasn't what the pros called 'Star of David' – north to south, east to west – but it did have its awkward weeks, and this was one of them. On the other hand, Dacai had a lively fan base, and the Polytechnic Hall was a cracking venue.

With Vikki next to him, Stevie settled himself into his favourite window seat at the table; after going over the Troilova accounts with her he started checking messages on his BlackBerry. The Groans didn't have broadband so anything coming from Charlie would be by text, and he was always hoping for good news of Sally. A lot of his songwriting was done on the BlackBerry, too, where no one could look over what he was doing and start giving him rhymes for 'banker'.

But first, they had to get out of Troilova: a left from the hotel, around the main square, and south along the road out of town – which wouldn't be quick. The traffic was thick and free-for-all; with lane-switching, cutting up, squirting through spaces, sudden braking, stop lights blazing and horns blaring. In Travonia if you got somewhere first you deserved to be there. But Kris the driver could win this sort of competition with the best, and he got applause from the crew by taking a lane arrowed for a right turn, steering straight ahead, and then driving the splitter through an amber traffic light.

And that was what saved No Rider. When the bomb

went up they were at a crossroads and three lanes of traffic away from the explosion, with a bus between them and the CFP terrorists' target. The flash seared into their eyes, the sound blitzed their eardrums – and suddenly everything was everywhere, twisted metal, shredded glass, flesh and blood flying around in a blast wave that rocked the van and vacuumed the air.

Somehow, Kris kept going, wheels losing traction for a few seconds as they lifted clear of the road.

'Hell!'

'Shit!'

'What was that?'

A front wheel punctured and the van tipped. The off-side passenger window crumbled to sugar, and through it came the shouts and screams of atrocity. Kris pulled over, everyone shaking. Stevie was first out, chasing back to the devastation of the square, Kris and Vikki close behind. Dead and injured lay in pools of blood, and a severed leg thumped onto a car bonnet. There was a hellish stench from Semtex and raw guts as shredded paper and torn clothing fell like flayed skin. Stevie suddenly vomited over a ripped-open body.

The rest of No Rider came running amid the shouting and screaming, the wailing and whimpering; 'I'm a doctor,' and 'Over here!' and, 'Viktor! Viktor!

Where are you?' Heads were cradled, hands held, and shirts torn up for bandages, until the emergency services arrived, driving across the grass of the central reservation – *Ambulanta, Politia and Pompierii*, their sirens sounding like the wailing of hell.

The professionals took over. Tape was rolled out, the wrecked taxi now a crime scene; tarpaulins and body bags hid the gruesome remains of people; and stretchers carried the injured into ambulances, and away. But nothing could ever erase the terrible images of death and destruction that fouled No Rider's minds.

An hour later Kris was taping up a cardboard replacement for the van window, while back in the bar of the Tuti Hotel the band was arguing among themselves.

'We go home. I could've stayed in my old country to get annihilated.' Sean O'Hara, in a clean shirt from his holdall, was hitting the Irish whiskey and thumping the table. 'I lost my old dad to a bomb, minding his own business in the Europa Hotel. I don't need this crap while I'm minding mine.'

Stevie said nothing, swilling his mouth with Diet Coke to get rid of the taste of vomit.

Nicky Harris shook his head. '"Go home"? My home's here, wi' you lads. The van, wharever hotel, wherever dressin' rooms, it's where I live.' For a big, hearty northerner he suddenly sounded like a lost kid. 'An' wha' do we go back to for six months? Eh? Summer festivals are all sorted – Reading, Glastonbury, Download, Leeds – an' campus gigs stop when the unis pack up. All we'll get is Black Pudding Galas an' Fag Pie Sundays…'

'What does the contract stipulate?' Paul Stoner asked Vikki. 'Do we get paid if we pull out?'

She was still in shock. She had cleaned up, too, and with her hair damp from the sink she looked more like a fresher than a tour manager. But she was ready for this. 'We are not paid direct in Travonia. We are paid by DMA Promotions, in sterling, to our agents…'

'But DMA must carry insurance on the tour…?'

'Let me read you.' Vikki pulled a copy of the contract from her satchel. '"Clause Seven – Decline to Perform. The Artiste reserves the right to decline to perform without prejudice to the full agreed fee in the event of any reason beyond the control of the Artiste including – but not limited to – strike, lock out, war, fire, or other Act of God, such as earthquake or serious or dangerous weather conditions."'

'We can say we got the wind up,' Deano said. But nobody laughed.

'You could argue it was an "Act of God",' Paul Stoner went on, slapping cash onto the bar for another beer. 'Think about it. Some political nutter—'

'Come on, man!' Winston's usually black face was still grey. 'How's a car bomb left by some political nutter an "Act o' God"?'

Stoner picked up his bottle and swigged. 'A nutter's as much an "Act of God" as a cyclone, right? If whatever we mean by God created the world, then that God created you an' me, an' saints, an' terrorists, an' nutters, didn't he?'

'You could argue it's war, civil war—'

'There's no bloody argument,' Stevie cut in. 'Did DMA and any of us say no to playing Camden KOKO after the embassy bomb? Did we pull out of the Roundhouse five days after Dover Street?'

Vikki shot a look at him, and nodded her support.

'The world's full of all this shit,' Stevie went on. 'Look at John Lennon. Where the hell can you go on this planet that guarantees you don't run up against a mental case? Not even normal Norway – look at that paranoid schizophrenic who shot up an island of students.'

'I'll give y'that – we cry off an' they've won,' Nicky said.

Sean O'Hara was shaking his head. 'It's not our war

to win. No Rider don't win or lose. These scum aren't after winning over us, we're not their enemy, we're just victims in the fall-out. Like mostly. Look at the police the last two nights. Were they at our load-in door? Neg, they were at the punters' way out. I tell you, there's a civil war brewin' here, an' our favourite move's gettin' our arses out of it while the airport's still open. My people's seen enough of all this stuff.'

'Mine, too,' Stevie said, quietly. 'Sally was badly damaged by a bomb like that.' He had to clear his throat. 'But did I run scared an' break us up?'

'Don' accuse me of running scared!' O'Hara's voice was shaking.

'Sorry. Bad choice of words.' Stevie blew out his cheeks. 'But let me remind you all – Vikki might be tour manager, and DMA might do the deals, but No Rider's my band, and it has been right from the off with Denny Drew.' His eyes took in each of them around the bar. 'We could get paid for not playing these two gigs in Dacai this week – mental stress, shock, call it what you like – Vikki can sort that, but I'm saying this tour goes on, all the way to the last gig…'

'You're on, Stevie.' From Deano Rivera.

'…And anyone who wants to go home can go home. I'll get sit-ins flown out for next week.'

O'Hara turned away and made to walk to the stairs – but he'd checked out that morning so he didn't have a room to go to. He came back.

Stevie went over and hugged the man, who suddenly looked lost. 'I know about your dad, and I know you're not running scared, mate. Not from getting killed. What a car bomb does is hurt you inside, more than any body wound. I know, and I know why you'd be going...'

O'Hara was crying now, the shock coming out.

'...But don't go, man. No Rider won't work without you, not the same – and nor will the tour.'

The Irishman had turned his face away from everyone.

Kris came into the bar, to a roomful of silence.

'Van is good,' he said.

'You OK to drive?'

'OK. Yes. Sure.'

'Then those who's coming, let's go,' said Stevie. 'And Vikki's got dosh for those who want to go to the airport.' He turned to O'Hara to look into his face.

There was a moment of hard thinking in the bar – ended by everyone filing out, and taking their seats again in the splitter, Sean O'Hara last, but included.

* * *

Maev Portland came down her flight of steps, walked along the pavement, came up Charlie's, and rang at the door. Charlie watched her all the way – she'd never done this before. Unless it was about the rattling boiler she always caught one of them in the street, or at the parking at the back. She'd never been into their place, and they'd never been into hers, not even for Christmas drinks. So, what was this? Was she on to him? Was his cover blown? Had some press creep told her that Sally Julien was in rehab or somewhere?

She rang again. Oh, God! What was he going to do: answer the door, or lie low and pretend to be out? But he'd been practising guitar and when he'd switched on, the amp had screeched with feedback. She had to know someone was in.

'Mile End Towers' was a weird conversion. The front door opened directly into the upstairs living room. The main bedroom and the bathroom were just along from it, and down a flight of stairs were the kitchen, Charlie's bedroom, the sound studio, and the door onto the patio. He'd come up here for the plectrum in his school bag, and when he'd looked through the window there was Maevy-baby, coming to ring.

She rang again.

So what was he going to do? Being here on his

own was getting dodgier every day. How long could he keep this up, living next door to an old newspaper reporter? He turned 360° for no reason at all, but as his head spun, inspiration suddenly hit him. Yes! He ran to the bathroom, kicked everything off, wrapped a towel around his waist, and shimmied fast to answer the door. He didn't want her coming back later.

'Hello.' He put his head round the woodwork, nearly letting the towel slip. 'Oops!'

'Oh, I'm sorry, Charlie. I've caught you at a bad time.'

'Sort of. Mum couldn't come to the door, she's gone into the shower after me.'

'Ah.'

'She's got to rush out to Croydon.'

Croydon? Where the hell did Croydon come from?

'Not to worry. It was just to tell her to watch Sky News.' Maevy-baby peered past him at the clock on the wall. 'It's Travonia…'

Charlie nearly dropped the towel for real. 'Why, what's up?'

'That's where your dad is, isn't it? Tell her to see the news…'

'Why? Is there a special reason?'

Maevy-baby narrowed her eyes, making some

decision. 'There's been a bomb. Probably nothing, but I think she should know...'

And so bloody well should I! 'OK. I'll watch for her, tell her about it—'

'You're a star.' And Maevy-baby went, Charlie checking her back to her own flat every step of the way before switching on Sky News; and way down the running order came the Travonia item – the newsreader on a split screen with a loop of pictures taken on a mobile phone.

'A car bomb exploded in the Travonian town of Troilova today, killing seven people and injuring thirty more. The atrocity happened outside the headquarters of the governing power, the Capitalist Freedom Party. Troilova is the birthplace of the country's president, Gheorghe Ardeleanu, and responsibility for the outrage has already been claimed by the dissident Neo-Vlach Party – also responsible for the London bombings – which is seeking its own separate state in the south of the country...'

God! Troilova rang a bell. Charlie left the news and rushed to his travel bag, pulling out his dad's tour sheet. And, shit, No Rider had played two gigs in the town, on Tuesday and Wednesday – with a two-day drive to Dacai for Friday and Saturday nights. *His dad had been due to leave Troilova that morning.* Charlie fumbled for his BlackBerry and texted him. It would be half-seven out there, but they wouldn't be in a concert venue tonight, today and tomorrow was travelling. *If they were anywhere on earth at all.*

And what a stupid thought that was! Everyone knew the first thing British news channels do in plane crashes or earthquakes is say if any Brits are caught up in it. A thousand poor devils can die in a foreign flood, but if one Brit gets his feet wet, that's the big story in the UK.

All the same, his dad hadn't texted – and he should have.

```
Just seen news of car bomb in Trav.
R U ok? Text back. Charlie.
```

But when Charlie's BlackBerry rang, it wasn't a text but his dad live.

'Charlie! Hi, Kid.'

'Dad. I've seen the news. Are you OK?'

'Sure. Course I am. It was some random nutter, all under control. We're in a nice little hotel taking a night off, eating potato soup and – what am I having next?' he asked someone.

'Tagliatelle.'

'Salmon and mushroom tagliatelle. What are the Groans giving you?'

Baked beans, like always. 'Er, Nan's done a risotto...' *Please God, Dad, don't break all records and ask to talk to her! And thank God the Groans hardly ever watched the news.*

'Anyway, just to know you're all right. I'm going to see Mum in a bit.'

'Great. I've had a word, still very quiet – but give her my love.'

'Will do. Cheers, then, Dad.'

'Cheers, Kid. Thanks for checking.'

'Take care.'

'What else?' And, click, the call was over.

Of course, Charlie hadn't dared ask his dad about any other man his mum might be feeling guilty about. But some of yesterday's swirling had cleared in his head and somehow he hadn't felt the need; he just knew his mum and dad were dead solid. Think about his dad's birthday, only a week before the bomb. It was his mother's idea. When his dad was out of the house they'd rehearsed their secret song – words by Charlie Peat, music by Sally Julien, played on acoustic guitar and sung by the pair of them. 'Homage to the Homme'.

'The homme of bonhomie,
The man of "nombreuse" smiles,
The partner, pal and "patron"
Puts on ten thousand miles.

'Twelve months added on his clock,
On the road and in our hearts,
"Bon anniversaire" to Stevie Peat,
King of Grove Road charts.'

Think of the trouble they'd taken to get it right – it had been top of his mum's agenda – and the tender way she'd sung the corny words; that could never have been an acting job, not even by a top performer like her. They came from her heart, and Charlie knew where that heart belonged. With his dad, no other chance.

So, tonight's mission was to probe her as gently as he could about the sort of person this mystery man might be because, if he'd come jumping out as something bugging her, he'd got to be found. And soon.

6

Goran Bucataru's mobile phone rang, the first line of an old Orthodox chant. He was sitting in the cab of a Challenger tractor, ploughing deep potato furrows into wet and heavy Lincolnshire soil to the sound of a heavy Christian cross clanking against the windscreen. He was in his sixties, and tough, having survived the Soviet years in Travonia. He'd been allowed to keep his farmland in the south by hiding his religion and setting up a commune to sell cheap crops to the communist government. He had worked hard and kept his family fed. But when the communists were driven out and Gheorghe Ardeleanu's Capitalist Freedom Party became 'The Power', Bucataru had been accused of collaborating with the hated Soviets. His land had been confiscated and sold to a Chinese-owned company – which was when he fled to England, where this Market Rasen farm had given him reasons for getting up in the mornings. As a skilled farmer he was in a good job, but he dearly wanted to be ploughing his own fields, instead of sending money home.

'Bucataru – you've heard the news?' Now this phone call from Rajov Tomescu was tapping some of that money.

'The bomb? Of course.' The men's hostel and the workers' club had been filled with talk of the Troilova explosion.

'We threatened it, didn't we? We promised you we were serious: London and Troilova – and with the big one still to come.'

'You made some promises…'

'We want you to know nothing's going to stop us from returning southern Travonia to its Orthodox roots.'

'But all the killing… I don't like killing.' Goran Bucataru held a steady line down the field.

'So tell me – what other means are there when our Christian faithful are locked up and tortured?'

Bucataru swung the tractor in a wide arc at the end of the two-thousand-acre field.

'…Hello – are you there?'

'I'm ploughing. With one hand. The soil's too heavy to stop this thing.'

'But you will make a donation to the cause? You can do it here and now. You have a bank card?'

Holding the Challenger steady, Bucataru checked that he'd got his wallet. 'Perhaps. Yes, all right. But on condition…'

'I'm sure we can meet whatever con—'

'...That you will guarantee my rights to my own land.'

The reply was immediate. 'Of course. I promise it in the name of the Lord Jesus, and of the Archbishop Boev. One big upset will send the Chinese scuttling. They'll do business with the Romanians instead of Ardeleanu, and the Power will lose its credibility. Our people will come out of the shadows all over the south, and other dissident groups will join in and attack the north.'

'You sound very sure of this.'

'We *are* very sure. So be with us; or you can plough your farmer's English fields until you're too old to hold his tractor in a straight line...'

Bucataru took a firmer grip.

'How much will you give, Goran? We need generosity. It's a wise investment in your future. Three thousand euros...?

The two South Travonians bartered and the deal was set up, a twenty-first-century transaction: electronic banking by a ploughman at his plough.

If it hadn't been for the unnerving feeling of something terrible always about to happen, Charlie felt like a regular Central-line commuter as he headed out to Debden. But he needed to be a regular – right now the help he could give his mother dominated his life. And how she was tonight was number-one important. Yesterday she'd been so many miles away he hadn't really known her. Before a big gig she sometimes wasn't the same person, not even to him, her Prince. Musicians were all different, he knew that. His dad was his dad all the time: he could be in the middle of a solo and still want to know who was going out for chips. But then the stuff he did was mostly fast rhythms and machine-gunned words; while she sang love songs, blues, gospel – emotional numbers that dug deeper into her soul.

Anyway, he was soon going to find out.

These Oyster fares weren't cheap – but he'd had just enough cash to buy her a dozen budding blue irises at the station. She loved blue irises; she had them in her dressing rooms all through their season. A few people on the tube smiled at him as if he was on his way to see a girlfriend, which would be nice one day: his mother better, and him and Francine on an evening out somewhere. But his mum wasn't near to being any better yet, so lose that thought, boy, lose it.

By the time he got to Debden the irises were starting to open – almost different flowers from the ones he'd bought at Mile End. And after a fast walk and a short search in the home he found his mother in the dining room, and gave them to her.

She was finishing her supper at a table with Bridget, who got up to go. 'If they're not for me, Charlie, I'm green with envy, and I'm away.'

'Sorry, Bridget.' But did his mother remember irises, and if she did, were they still her favourites; or would they get the fruit jellies and chocolate treatment?

'Sit down.' She was eating apple and custard like someone at school dinners, not wasting a lick. Coming off that tablet seemed to be giving her an appetite. She took the flowers, held them, admired them. 'Prince, they're lovely.'

Great! She liked the irises, and she'd called him "Prince".'

'Who sent them?'

'Me. I bought them.' Not some fan. *And not some other man.*

'Very nice.' She put them in her water glass.

'Have you finished, Mum?'

'Yes.' She got up, seeming a bit more sure of herself tonight, just a glimpse of the old Sally Julien – but in spite of the 'Prince' it was of the old on-tour singer, not the old mum.

'Fancy a walk outside?'

'Not now.' And she didn't move, still standing awkwardly with her chair tipped back behind her. 'Have you found him?' she asked, as direct as Dr Leigh.

'Found *who*, Mum?'

'Ronnie.' Her eyes were wide, like, *Who else?*

'Ronnie?'

'Piano.' She mimed fingers on a keyboard. 'Ronnie Moreton.'

'Oh, Ronnie…' Ron Moreton was a top jazz pianist rather than an accompanist – but when his mother could get him, he was the best. Other people played her accompaniments off the sheet; he turned them into real jazz.

She still hadn't moved her feet, instead she was leaning on the dining table, fingers almost bent backwards, her eyes staring into his as big as he'd ever seen them.

'I need Ronnie.'

'Of course you do, he's your best man at the piano. Just get you better and back on the road, and—'

'Find him, Charlie!'

'Certainly. Sure.' So *Ron Moreton* was this man she wanted, as simple and as obvious as that. And it was bloody marvellous if that meant she was thinking about the future. 'I'll try. I'll do my best.'

She smiled at him, her body still at that odd angle, but

her face so full of grace. 'Thank you.' And she walked away from the supper table, clutching her blue irises to her chest.

Charlie watched her go, and nodded his head as if he'd just heard one of those lyrics that tell you more than the words. His life these past few weeks had been driven by just making sure that he saw her, and saw her – and by telling serious lies and risking broken friendships to do so. But it had all been part of his desperation to get her better, if only by being there with his love. Now he had a target. She wanted him to find Ron Moreton, one of the best-known names in the business. Well, now the name was out, that wasn't going to be too hard to do, was it?

If only he could do it before his world blew up again.

Zanko Boev sat at the kitchen table in the Tottenham safe house; except, as he told the others, it wasn't such a safe house any more. He was shaking his head and cursing into a bowl of thick leek soup.

'It may not be us,' he said. 'We may not be the Neo-Vlach activists who get to lead the New Power, not if we're caught – but whoever it is, the revolution has to happen first.'

'True.' Rajov Tomescu spoke through a big mouthful.

'We've got to be on our toes. British Intelligence is on high alert. I'm getting tell-tale clicks even on the pay-as-you-go phones.' The others looked at the man with soup on his chin. 'Perhaps bombing in London was a mistake. Our workers here are also getting these noises on their cellphones. My guess is, British security is monitoring all network calls spoken in our language.'

'So why don't you speak something else?' Stoica sneered. 'You're fat enough for two people, let the second person be French.'

Zanko Boev growled at the banter. 'The London bombs were to encourage our southern people; and the Neo-Vlach have claimed responsibility for Troilova. But they were small scale only. Everything is wasted if we don't carry out the big, final attack. The means to do it is ordered – but not yet paid for. So we carry on finding the funds – but from some other premises before the British find us.' He held the other two with his archbishop eyes. 'We have to scare off the Chinese, so we must not be found before the stadium attack.'

Tomescu looked away and wiped his bowl with a thick slice of soda bread. 'They'd have to be very lucky to find us just yet. There's a million people in this part of London. Three quarters of them carry cellphones. Many of them don't speak English. Right now these eavesdroppers would need the sort of luck that wins a lottery.' He cut himself another slice.

'It's not *human* eavesdroppers, fool.' Otto Stoica got up. 'It's computer linguistic recognition they use. They've got a million bytes spying on your million people.'

'Then what about going to Remes, in Kent? He does everything in good English, perfect accent – and he's a good way out of London.'

Boev shook his head – out of the question. 'He owns his house, lives like an Englishman, comes and goes with our money and our needs. He's making passports for our flight home. That man is too crucial and too clean to be compromised; going to Kent can only be a last resort. No, we keep our heads down but our eyes open. We need somewhere else with a landline connection we can open up…'

'So what sort of place is that?'

'Another shop without a tenant, different from this…'

Stoica nodded, and took Tomescu's bowl from him. 'And you, Fat Man, had better start learning some French.'

At which none of them laughed. Instead, Archbishop Boev stood, and led them in a short prayer for an Orthodox Christian success.

* * *

Charlie was proud of his callused fingers, caused by constant pressing and sliding on steel strings; they made him feel worthy of owning two guitars. So which of the two should he take to the Rubber Girders audition tonight? For the full rock-and-roll sound the Fender Stratocaster he'd been given on his fifteenth birthday would be better. But, living his lie next door to Maevy-baby, he didn't play it so often these days; it was too tempting to let rip, even in the studio downstairs. Indoors he mostly used his Tanglewood elecoustic. He could play that the same way as an acoustic, and plug it into an amp when he wanted more oomph – which meant he wasn't so good on the Stratocaster these days. But after swinging this way and that he went for it, anyway. Its 'fiesta red' looked more flashy, more pro, and the tremolo arm would give a bit of reverberation.

He was getting jumpier and jumpier about his audition, but the thought of finding Ron Moreton was also churning his insides up. His mother needed to see the man, but he knew that wouldn't be anything to do with performing again, not yet; it was more likely something coming out of Dr Leigh's therapy sessions – getting her to remember more about the night of the bomb. Dead important stuff. The trouble was, how soon could he get in touch with Ron? It hadn't been as straightforward as

do. He'd start with Dire Straits' 'Twisting by the Pool', which was a good settler, not too heavy. He'd notch things up with the Manics' 'So Why So Sad?'; and then he'd go straight into a big finish, 'Everything is Average Nowadays' by the Kaiser Chiefs – just to show how above-average Charlie Peat was!

He practised and practised these three until his fingers hurt and time ran out, and with his stomach looping the loop he headed off for Bow Road station. This was it. This was when he was going to pretend he wasn't Stevie Peat's son.

The Rubber Girders had use of the music room at Tudor Hart Community College, where Pete Snowdon's mother was Head of Cultural Studies, and they could make as much noise as they liked.

According to Francine, Pete was now at Greenwich University doing Education Studies, but his heart was in the band, getting them gigs around the East End and out into Essex and Kent, with Rubber Girders making a name for giving students a good night out. So finding a really good new rhythm guitar was going to be crucial to him.

Charlie walked along to Bow Road station. Whenever he saw that girl she lifted his spirits, although with him on his mission for his mother she'd complicated the twisting inside him – guilt for daring to feel 'up'. Francine had style, and she came up from the platforms in a black suit with a huge scarlet rose on the lapel, looking like Anna Sinkovská's sister. *Wow!*

'Hiya, France.'

'Charlie-boy.'

She was the only one who called him that, and it always fizzed him.

'You look very—'

She cut him off. 'You all right?'

'Sure.' Although he wasn't.

'What're you going to play?' She started leading the way to the college.

Bijan was right. Getting somewhere or making any sort of choice, she did the navigating. He hadn't texted her the way he might have done, but he wanted her to like what he'd decided to do.

'"Twisting by the Pool", "So Why So Sad?" and "Everything is Average Nowadays".' He looked at her for the nod.

'I know "So Sad" for playing, shall I come in on it? Not at first – after I've picked up your rhythm?'

'Be my guest.'

She walked on fast. She was a good leader; Charlie

knew where he was going with her, and tonight it was great to have her taking charge. They went to the back of the main college building and along an open walkway towards a smaller complex; Charlie's pulse went from reggae beat to ska as they walked on towards the sound coming from the studios – the thump of a rhythm on percussion and bass.

'You'll be great.'

'Will I?' The thing was, all these Rubber Girders knew about was No Rider, so Charlie had a lot to live up to. These people would be quick to mark him down if he wasn't brilliant.

'You're *you*. If they want you, they want *you*, not your dad's son.' Francine had read his mind. She could do that – a bit like his mother.

'I know – and you keep telling me.' He looked around him. 'This way? Which way is it?' He was talking gibberish and he knew he would be for the next half-hour.

'Through here.'

The beat coming from the music room now had a tune laid on top of it – 'I Got Your Number' by the Stereophonics – and Charlie could pick out the line of the rhythm guitar.

'Ray's still with us, till the end of the summer…'

Francine was inside his head again.

'That's right.' Still the monkey talk. His fret fingers tingled with a sudden weakness, as if the calluses had sheered off and he was a raw beginner again. 'This way, is it?'

'This way, Charlie-boy.' And she stopped, and faced him, and suddenly kissed him on the lips. 'You're going to be totally great.'

Which was when his case strap slipped off his shoulder, and he had to swoop to save his guitar.

'Dynamite!' he said – which wasn't gibberish, although he wished he hadn't chosen that actual word...

7

'Deano – what's the time in England?'

'Party time. Eightish.' Deano went on polishing his dark glasses.

'Think golden thoughts for Charlie, then. He's trying for a place in a band.' Stevie was in the poky bar at the Capsa Hotel in Tinnu, No Rider's halfway house on the road to Dacai. He'd eaten his tagliatelle, had a lie on his bed, and come along the corridor for a nightcap.

'He's not after living this life of crap, is he?' Sean O'Hara asked.

'Who knows with kids? It's what he thinks he wants.'

O'Hara looked down at his cloudy whiskey, which wasn't even Scottish, let alone Irish. 'It's an age thing, Stevie. This is a great life till you're thirty – sleeper buses where no one sleeps, sex an' drugs an' sausage rolls – but there comes a time, my friend, when you look at tonight's bed, an' it's the same bed as last night's, an' you say, "Sweet Jesus – I thank you very much."'

'You're saying this is your last tour, then?' Deano wanted to know.

'Could be.' O'Hara took a sip and grimaced. 'The

grand Celebration Concert could well be Sean O'Hara's swan-song.'

There was a short silence, like a mark of respect. The Irishman had been with No Rider forever.

'Celebration duck shoot, more like,' Deano said, peeved. 'Us – at a government flag-wag? We've seen how their Gestapo like our fans…'

'No. They need us there,' Vikki told him.

Stevie swigged his local beer. 'Forget duck shoot – that gig's got charity gala written all over it. The Travonia Army Choir, the Naraiova Philharmonic Orchestra, the Transylvania Pops, some opera singer, and we're second on the bill to a troupe from the Chinese State Circus. Tasters for everyone, but no feast.'

'The acrobats'll go arse over tit among the amps and stands.'

'But it's a trade deal celebration paying big bread. On state television.'

Deano leant over and patted Stevie's arm. 'Shall we write 'em a special song? Call it "Filthy Yen" and feel better about it?'

'Like to. Except we won't get a work permit next time. Vikki's right, they need us, we're their safety valve.' Stevie dropped his voice as if the barman might be a secret agent. 'They're not stupid. They know who comes to our concerts, and their thinking is, if No Rider's on the bill it'll keep any hotheads quiet...'

'How moral is that? It's like the Jewish "Come Dancing" team gigging for Adolf Hitler.'

Stevie shrugged. 'We're on a contract. We signed up to this deal before we realised how rotten this lot is. And look on the upside. This concert's worth six months' work, we're not back out here till the autumn – and we're bashing out our astringent stuff for twenty minutes on state television. That can't be bad.'

'Could be a title for a new song.' O'Hara held his glass up to the light, and frowned. 'God save Mother Riley, I think this really *is* piss—'

The others looked at the glass.

'—So tell your Charlie to turn round three times an' think real hard about life on the long an' pot-holed road, a hundred miles from a decent whiskey.'

Stevie nodded, and looked at his BlackBerry as if he was willing it to ring with good news. 'As long as he does himself justice. No one can ask for anything more.'

Charlie had met the band after a couple of gigs with Francine, and he liked them. Ray Stevens, the rhythm guitar who'd be leaving at the end of the summer, pulled out his own jack and plugged in Charlie's Stratocaster.

He backed-up on lyrics, too, and there was an SM58 mic in front of his position that was about right for height. But Charlie hadn't planned on singing tonight. Francine gave him an E from her keyboard, and he did what he hoped seemed like a quick, professional tune-up. He looked around the band. He was ready.

'What're you going to do?' Pete asked. 'We'll come in if we know it.'

'And we'll come in if we don't!' Francine was a great smoother.

'I thought, "Twisting by the Pool" for starters…'

'Dire Straits. Fine.'

Charlie took a deep breath, set his fingers on the frets for the opening chord, and counted himself in. *One, two, three, four…*and off he went on the eighties hit single, his neck too rigid and his right shoulder too hunched, but overall keeping himself together. He had played the number better; nerves, a slippery plectrum, everything a bit uncertain; but it didn't go too badly, and he didn't hit any bum notes so he wasn't going to be too hard on himself. There wasn't a player in the world who wouldn't be nervous at a first try-out. He didn't wait for any verdict, though, he didn't want it yet. Bouncing off the final chord of 'Twisting' he went straight into the intro of 'So Why So Sad?' – and he was better with this heavier number, there was less time to think. Now his heartbeat was slowing to normal, his breathing was coming easier, and he was beginning to enjoy himself, knowing he looked more relaxed and professional. The Rubber Girders were upping their sound, more of them coming in, and Francine's keyboard line came across loud and steady, as if she was holding his hand. And while everyone was reverbing the final note of 'So Why So Sad?' he suddenly hit 'Everything is Average Nowadays'. Within seconds they were all in on it, full on, Rubber Girders doing their thing, with Charlie Peat on rhythm guitar.

It was great, and as 'Everything is Average' came to its drum-thumping end, without thinking about it he suddenly stepped up to Ray's mic and went into a song the Rubber Girders definitely wouldn't know.

'I'll sing something sweet in a voice from the grinder,
Take you to heaven on a rocky ride,
Kiss you, my love, and fight like a minder,
Hard-edge the world from my soft inside.
Inside out,
Inside out,
Out the inside,
Inside out.'

The others started picking up the tune, and Ray Stevens plugged himself into a spare amp.

> *'But it's the people sitting in tanks and fighters,*
> *And figures in banks making governments fall,*
> *It's a powerful finger with the lightest touch*
> *Who softly triggers the end of it all.*
> *Inside out,*
> *Inside out,*
> *Out the inside,*
> *Inside out.'*

'I like it!' Ray shouted, playing rhythm an octave up on Charlie.

> *'Don't think power's all muscle and might,*
> *Don't think Semtex blows off its own doors,*
> *It's the work of a bigot whose poisonous spite*
> *Detonates hatred to further a cause.*
> *Inside out,*
> *Inside out,*
> *Out the inside,*
> *Inside out.'*

They played the rest of the song through another verse and chorus.

'Great! Where's that come from?'

Charlie took off his guitar and stood it on Ray's stand. 'Me. I wrote it.'

Francine looked more surprised than anyone. 'I love it. Is it totally yours?'

'Stevie's never even heard it,' Charlie said – and the forbidden name was out in the open. To be ignored, of course.

'I didn't mean that, Charlie-boy...'

'Do you know "I Got Your Number"?' Pete Snowdon asked him, moving on.

'I'll have a go.' Right now it seemed there was nothing Charlie couldn't *not* do. He picked up his guitar again as the band went into the Stereophonics' song, and, watching Ray's chords and fingering, he came in, too. They played that number and a whole songbook until the caretaker came to send them home, when there were smiles all round, and a pat on the back from Pete.

'I'll text you, Charlie.'

'Cheers.'

Francine was sparkling as they walked to the tube. 'You were ace, Charlie-boy, I was really proud.'

'Still didn't get a dive bomb in...' He looked rueful, but he didn't mean it.

'You and your Jimi Hendrix dive bomb! Be yourself – because I loved your song, you secret devil. You never told me...'

There's a lot I haven't told you. And I should, I really should...

' "I'll sing something sweet in a voice from the grinder, take you to heaven on a rocky ride..." Memorable stuff.'

The Stratocaster wasn't nearly so heavy now. Charlie might soon be a Rubber Girder – and Francine had kissed him and was walking along holding his hand: the fret hand with the callused fingers. For a couple of hours at least, things seemed on the up.

Vikki Basescu's mobile phone rang with a surprise. They were in the splitter when Ruthie Lewis-Evans from Channel Four News got through to say that she was in Travonia in advance of Four's coverage of the Celebration Concert on the sixth of May. Right then she was in Naraiova researching the Chinese deal for Travonian Black Sea minerals, and Four News was going to do a series of segments in the run-up to the Chinese trade visit. They wanted to get some lively studio debate about European Union competition for Chinese money. She poured out the details to Vikki as if no other story could ever be so important. Their series would include shots of the state celebration at the Dynamo Naraiova Stadium and, seeing that the British band No Rider was on the bill, they'd like to do an interview with Stevie Peat.

Pressing mute, Vikki filled Stevie in and passed him the phone.

'Hi. I'm Ruthie Lewis-Evans from Channel Four.'

'I'm Stevie Peat from the back of a splitter.'

'I'll come straight to it, Stevie. Our anchor Will Palmer would like to interview you down the line from Dacai…' She left a pause for Will Palmer's name and fame to register.

'Will Who?'

'Will Palmer. He presents Four News.'

'Ah.'

'And your promoters say you're at Dacai this weekend. I can get there with a crew on Sunday if you'd give us half an hour.'

'What's the fee on the table?'

'On top of the free publicity? That's not up to me, I'm afraid.'

'Never is. No prob. I can do Sunday – but not too early.'

'Great. We'll probably run the interview on Monday

night, one of our first packages. Other times we'll have coverage of the Troilova bomb and a profile of their PM.'

'Haven't you got enough news without this Travonia stuff? It's a sad old country, you know…'

Ruthie Lewis-Evans had it all off pat. 'The Chinese economic influence in Travonia is very big news. Critics say it's exploiting poorly paid miners; and political economists say that by making Travonia rich, the Chinese are downgrading the EU countries in the area.'

'This place doesn't look very rich to me. Ask the punters who come to our concerts.'

'That's well on the cards, too. There's a radical student element that might affect Chinese opinion, and your thoughts on the people who come to No Rider concerts would be of great interest to our viewers.'

'I doubt that; but I'll give it a go. Anyway, talk about the set-up with Vikki – she's a hard woman. And I'll see you on Sunday.'

The text when it came beat the ring at the doorbell by thirty seconds – hardly time for Charlie to do a jig around the kitchen table.

```
How about rhythm guitar with the RG?
Pete.
```

Fantastic! He was in! He was in the band! Rubber Girders wanted him. In the time it took him to read the text a couple of times over, his insides calmed and he was the old Charlie Peat, head up and ready to wink into a mirror. But there was no time to send a reply to Pete before he answered the door. If it was Maevy-baby he mustn't be a phantom. He tried to think fast as he ran up the stairs and along the corridor. Where was his mother supposed to be today? Shopping? That would be favourite on a Saturday morning – before she went over to Croydon again...

But, *oh God!* – when he opened the door who was standing there holding one of his hold-alls? Grandad Groan!

'Helloah, boy! How's our Charles?' He ruffled Charlie's hair with a big hand.

Charlie actually *was* Charlie; 'Charlie' was the name on his birth certificate, but the Groans had never settled for anything other than Charles.

'Where's your daddy?' Being family, Granddad Groan was already through the door, standing in the middle of the room looking all around him.

'He's had to go over to Croydon.'

'Not keeping you too straight indoors, is he?' Granddad Groan was staring at Charlie's clothes thrown over an armchair. The Groans' strict religious beliefs had it that the Good Lord was into every cupboard in the house – as well as into every corner of a boy's mind. They were on about tidiness all the time, whatever he was doing. *'Keep that page of homework neat, Charles. That scribble you've got on that paper there shows cluttered thinking. A mucky page reveals a mucky mind, and we're after good grades from you, my boy.'*

'I've brought the things you left behind, Charles – we can't have them cluttering the house for ever.'

Charlie had left in a hurry, after the last time they'd stopped him from going out to Debden. 'Thanks very much.'

'And this. Let your daddy see this. He was in Travonia before he came home, wasn't he?'

'Yeah.'

'The word, boy, is "Yes".' Grandad Groan produced a neatly folded sheet of *Daily Mail* from an inside pocket. It looked as if it had been ironed. 'Let him have a look at that. I don't want it back. He was right to come home from such a godforsaken place to look after his family. Even in his own fashion.' He handed the cutting to Charlie.

Charlie took it, anxious for the man to go. The last thing he wanted was to be asked for a glass of water, or a cup of coffee. To Grandad Groan, descending into the state of the kitchen, it would seem like going down into hell. And it would make him ask serious questions about whether his dad was actually back home.

'I can't stay, boy.'

'That's a shame.'

'And before you ask, your Nanna is well, and she asks me to give you her love.'

'Thanks.' Charlie tried to look grateful. 'And Mum sends her love to you both.' He wasn't going to let Grandad win any politeness victory.

'You've seen her recent?'

Charlie nodded without going into any details.

'Your Nanna and I don't do any good out there, we only seem to stir up her devils. And you're best keeping out of too much of that atmosphere, Charles. Let the good Lord do his work.'

The man looked sad. He could have made a good old grandad, Charlie reckoned, except for the Church of St Thomas, Leytonstone. He was a big, roly-poly man who'd have been great at romps – if he hadn't been so worried about disturbing the cushions. Now he hovered in the doorway for just a moment – and Charlie began to wonder if he might really have come for a word with his dad about money. The Groans had looked after him for those weeks and they hadn't taken a penny – although they'd always said they wanted nothing.

'That shirt could do wi' seein' the iron before you're seen in the street, boy.' And then he was gone.

Charlie took a look at the clock. He was meeting Bijan near West Ham station in forty-five minutes. Then it was out to Debden. But he'd got to reply to Pete Snowdon – and he definitely had to read this *Daily Mail* clipping in his hand.

He opened it up from its folding into precise thirds.

HUNT FOR IMMIGRANT BOMBERS

British anti-terrorist police are reporting some progress in their hunt for the three remaining Travonian immigrant extremists believed to be hiding in London. Their Orthodox Christian party has claimed responsibility for the recent bombings in the capital.

Sources close to the man-hunt say they are also wanted for questioning by their own government in connection with a car bomb planted outside the offices of the Travonian premier Gheorghe Ardeleanu in

his home town of Troilova. It killed thirteen and injured twenty-nine innocent people – nine seriously.

It is believed the attack was masterminded on British soil and was part-funded by immigrant workers in Britain and Europe.

When caught, Zanko Boev (58), Rajov Tomescu (49) and Otto Stoica (36) will be deported under guard to face questioning in their own country.

This latest atrocity underlines the need for greater control of Britain's national borders.

Charlie had seen the map of Travonia. It was a huge country. His dad stood more chance of being bombed in London than he ever would out there. He put the cutting into a drawer. The minor conflict he had to think about right now was the West Ham–Chelsea tie in the Cup replay a couple of weeks away. To keep things looking normal to Bijan he definitely needed to go; it would be unthinkable that he wouldn't. The Groans had never stopped him from going to a football match.

Tickets went on sale at twelve. He met up with Bijan only ten minutes late, having stopped in Green Street where there was a good signal to text his dad with his good news about Rubber Girders – and to ask if he knew Ron Moreton's contact details. Bijan pulled back his sleeve to look at his pilots' chronograph. 'You all right, Chas?'

'Sure. Had to wait a while at Mile End. Broken-down train.'

Bijan gave him a look. 'Mile End? Always gonna be a late boy, aren't you, if you get from Leytonstone to West Ham by way of Mile End. Don't ever ask to be my navigator.'

Charlie smacked himself inside his head. Stupid! He'd got to do better than this. He always took great care getting home from college, catching the bus towards Leytonstone first, then changing.

'Dropped in at home to check the mail.'

Bijan looked at Charlie's empty hands. 'Nil result, then?'

Charlie shook his head. 'Nothing important.' Bijan was needle sharp; he'd definitely got to up his act if he wasn't going to get caught out. The last thing he could afford was to be shot straight back into the clutches of the Groans.

They walked towards the Boleyn ground. West Ham was playing away to Arsenal that afternoon so it wasn't like a match day with supporters starting to fill the pavements. All the same, the queue for loyal old Roy Seboa's testimonial tickets stretched out of the car park and up the road. Charlie tried to enjoy the matey queue with all the talk about team selections, and form, and the importance of league points above everything else – everyone up for the same side. Walking the streets at away games could be scary, but here he was in, in, in – except that he was on one hell of a different wavelength from all these others. It was painful even remembering the kiss Francine had given him the night before. Nothing of this today or of last night was what his life was about right now. There was only one thing driving him, forever there in his head and in his gut: his mother getting better – and him doing anything on God's earth to help it happen.

Saturday morning, and on a normal day he'd buy his testimonial ticket and go home to one of his mum's salad lunches, the sort she always ate before a gig. But what would her day be like today, out at Debden? She'd be staring at the walls in her little cell as she ate off her pull-out table; or she'd be head-down in the dining room among all those sick and sad cases: all because of those bastard terrorists.

Mouthing the words, he joined in the queue singing

8

Charlie showed his mother his testimonial ticket – and she chucked his chin and said, 'Hope it's a good game, Prince.' She was calmer today, and he told her his plan to go to Bernie Jacobs' office on Monday to get Ron Moreton's address.

'I can't find his address in your book.' But he didn't want her to worry about it. 'And Dad says he hasn't got it.'

'He doesn't know Ron Moreton's business. Ron's mine.' She kissed Charlie. 'You find Ron Moreton,' she said, nodding hard. 'Find Ronnie.'

She was different again today; somehow she was more settled now that Ron Moreton's name was out in the open, released from her frozen memory. Her eyes looked at him with a trusting instead of an insistent look; softer, not so staring. And that put its own pressure on him. She thought finding Ron was in safe hands – but he'd still got to do it, hadn't he? The way life was going these days that might not be as easy as it seemed.

For an hour's relief from everything going on he sat down that night ready for the football highlights – when

Travonia suddenly poked its nose into the flat again. On *Match of the Day*.

'And there's added drama in the London derby at the Emirates,' they promised in the intro, and that was the first match they showed: the Hammers getting hammered four-nil. But the drama wasn't in the rubbish way they played. The big, shock-horror highlight the pundits condemned was the fight on the pitch. All three of their voices went up an octave at the sight of West Ham's Mikel Muresan and captain Stefan Caramitru standing and knocking hell's bells out of each other in the West Ham goalmouth.

'He's said something.'

'Yeah, Muresan's said something, an' Caramitru's got out of his pram.'

'Hit him on the penalty spot!'

'That weren't "handbags", that was assault...'

'Ref had no option.'

'No option at all. They both had to walk.'

'There'll be police charges, got to be.'

'Disgraceful. That's got no place on a Premier League pitch.'

'None whatsoever.'

But the final comment from manager Harry South was the one that hit home. 'That's not about football, it's all about politics,' he said. 'That's Travonian civil war, for sure.'

Civil war! The words hit Charlie like shrapnel. There wasn't just trouble in Travonia, there was civil war, and his dad was out there in the middle of it, pooh-poohing that bomb the other day; but he'd been in the town where it went off, the very town. And he had to be out there. Charlie really had checked the post that morning – and two of the regular statements were a current bank balance and the Stage Left account, where it was plain to see from the charges that his mother would soon be out of the place if his dad didn't keep earning on the tour. Stevie always said it was in the Peat musicians' DNA that they lived from tour to tour, sometimes from gig to gig; he reckoned it was what made them different, gave them an edge. But that edge would be well-blunted if he was forced out of the Travonia tour. It would take a long time for Bernie Jacobs to put another string of decent gigs together – and that could be a big knock-back for his mother out at Debden. Like a soldier in a war, his dad had got to serve his time in Travonia – for her to stay where she was with Dr Leigh, who seemed to be making a bit of progress.

But *civil war*! Charlie's history course at college made no bones about how bloody civil war could be.

*   *   *

Stevie did the Channel Four interview at half past ten, after a rousing Saturday-night gig. And things kicked off straight away when Palmer asked Stevie to comment on Saturday's incident at the Emirates Stadium.

'West Ham lost four-nil.' Stevie put on a gloomy face for the camera. 'What do you want me to say? I'm gutted. But what's that got to do with——?'

'You haven't heard? West Ham's two Travonian players stood on the pitch and fought tooth and nail, a real fight, till they were separated by their clubmates.' Will Palmer's voice on the satellite line sounded weird and tinny in the hotel lounge. 'They're banned from talking to the media, but the word is, it was all to do with Travonian politics.'

'Well, don't ask me. I've been busy. I only knew the score.'

'Apparently they're on two different sides politically. One player supports the government, the other justifies the use of Neo-Vlach terrorist tactics to free the south.'

'Well, I'm not burning a candle for anyone, but no one can ever justify terror. We're human beings, we have to find civilised ways of making change. That's the path our fans would take, I'm sure of that – who aren't Neo-Vlachs, so far as I know...'

'Would American slaves ever have been freed without civil war?'

'African slaves. You're right – and I can make a case for some wars as well – but I can't make a case for the sort of violence that's intended to scare the shit out of people, and kills, and ruins innocent victims' lives.'

'Don't some of your songs wind people up to take action? "Up the ante!"? Don't your send-ups ever inflame passions?'

Stevie stared into the camera and slowly shook his head. 'My lyrics are intended to inflame the passion to wave and stamp and boogie-woogie in the aisles. That's all. They're songs, Will, words that go with tunes.'

'Like "Mack the Knife" is just a song?'

'A send-up of an old opera, showing violence in a bad light. Wit, and satire, they're always the sharpest weapons.'

'Do you think all your fans would agree with you?'

Stevie gave it a couple of beats. 'Probably not. There's a lot wrong out here – but you'd have to ask them, wouldn't you? How should I know what party cards they carry in their back pockets?'

'Fair enough, but—'

'Look, I write songs and perform them. They come to gigs and listen to them. I work while they play. They go home to clean their apartments, I go back to a crap hotel while my own place in London gathers dust and cobwebs and the post piles up. But that's what I do, that's the deal. And when the show's over, that's the end of the deal, unless they want to buy a CD. They do whatever they do next day, and I ride off into the sunrise. Two sides of the equation – and, speaking for No Rider, they're the only two sides.'

'Won't some of your fans be disappointed to see you performing at the Chinese Celebration Concert?'

Stevie sighed. 'Listen, Will, I'm sure you ask some pretty shite questions on TV every night. Whether it's Channel Four for you or a big promoter for me, someone pays us both to do our professional jobs. And my job is to entertain: it's how I make my living. The only relationship between No Rider and any section of the audience is us playing for them and them listening to us.'

'Is that so? Can you really hide behind only being a performer when your strings are being pulled by an ultra-capitalist right-wing paymaster? Doesn't your integrity come into it? Where's your radical credibility now?'

'I doubt if you know what "radical" means.'

'I know "integrity", though. Stevie Peat of No Rider

– thank you very much.' And Will Palmer cut the interview there.

Ruthie Lewis-Evans and her crew didn't hang around for long, either. They struck their gear, asked for some signed T-shirts for their kids, and headed off to their rooms in a superior hotel.

And Stevie walked into the Novotel bar.

'What's got you all rowan-berried in the face?' O'Hara asked him.

'Bloody West Ham! The club finds out too late they've signed two warring Travonians. What's their scouting staff up to?'

The Irishman nodded wisely. 'That's why Glasgow Celtic is Glasgow Celtic, Glasgow Rangers is Glasgow Rangers, and you'd never put money on a Belfast United now, would you?'

Stevie shook his head; but slower and with less focus to his eyes than he normally would at the politics of football.

Charlie went to see his mother again that Sunday, but it was different from a midweek visit; there were more people there, the dining room and the grounds were dotted with relatives and friends, even the lounge was occupied with a church service. The only quiet, personal space was in her room, so they sat there holding hands, him determined not to bring up Ron Moreton's name unless he had to. He was going to Bernie Jacobs' office next day, when he hoped to find out some crucial stuff, but he couldn't be sure he'd even get in to see him. Meanwhile, he tried to keep the talk day-to-day, told his mother what he'd played at the Rubber Girders audition, went on about the No Rider tour and the audiences they'd had, and made up a load of lies about the Groans and their church activities, anything to be as normal as possible – which was totally out of the question. 'Normal' would have been her getting ready for a Sunday-night gig, the sort of shows she liked best where the venues weren't so big and the audiences were specialist, digging out old jazz numbers, going over tricky phrases, drumming hard-to-remember lyrics into her head. Against which, here they were, mid-afternoon, out in the Essex countryside with the sounds of an organ and some spidery singing coming up from the ground floor, guffaws of laughter at old showbiz tales coming in through the window, and the two of them talking down in their throats, the room tasting stale when it should have been acid-sharp with a Sunday-night gig to come. 'So Sad' – forget the Everley Brothers or Manic Street Preachers – he could write his own lyrics to a title like that.

'Ronnie Moreton!' The name suddenly cut the quietness as her head jerked back.

'Sure, Ronnie Moreton.'

'You won't let me down, will you?' Her hand holding his had tightened with that grip from the other day. He looked into her face. It was like a kid's, pleading with him to help her.

'I won't let you down, Mum. And then we're going to enjoy a million sunsets again.' Up to now he'd managed not to cry in front of her, but this moment brought him very close to it. It was as if she was the child sitting here in this pathetic state and he was the parent expected to be a sort of Father Christmas and bring her the present she wanted.

'I promise I won't let you down. I'll find him, you bet –' when the Peats had never been into gambling, and right then none of them was on anything like a winning streak.

Charlie had been to Bernie Jacobs' offices before. The 'shop', as Jacobs always called it, was on the second floor of a building in Denmark Street, reached through a dull door at the side. A dusty brass plate said 'Jacob Artistes' above a small entry phone. Charlie had a job to hear any reply after he'd pushed the buzzer – the street was narrow and busy – but a slight click of the door encouraged him to push it, and it gave.

Upstairs, a small reception area was hung with framed posters and performers' pictures – there was one of No Rider and a smaller one of Sally among them – with a desk set square in front of Jacobs' private office.

The receptionist, a middle-aged man with dyed hair and tinted glasses, looked up. He waved at a low sofa. 'I'm Brian.'

'Hi. I'm Charlie Peat, Stevie Peat's son…'

'Hi. Is our Stevie still wowing them – wherever he is?'

'Travonia. He's in Travonia.' *Surely the man should know that?*

'Of course he is. I've got a friend who went there once. Couldn't get a latte for cash or kindness. So what can we do for Stevie…?'

'For Mum. For Sally Julien.'

'Ah. And how's our lovely lady?'

As if you give a flying fart! Charlie was sure no one from the agency had been to see his mother at Stage Left, and her 'get well' card looked as if it had been signed by a rubber stamp.

'She's not too bad. But about her – I've come in on the off-chance Mr Jacobs can spare me a few minutes…'

'I'll see what I can do.' He made it sound a top favour. 'Perhaps just five minutes. He's got Diana Dean with him *pro tem*' – said in hushed tones – 'but I'll give him a little tinkle afore too long. Do sit.'

The telephone rang, releasing Charlie. He sat on the sofa and looked at an old copy of the *New Musical Express*, doing what musicians always did with trade papers, running a name-check. But it was all chart successes and the internationals who were making waves at the O2. He might have found something about No Rider, but he knew there'd be nothing about Sally Julien. The story agreed with the agency was that she was taking a couple of months out – nothing unusual. Charlie went right through it, read a couple of stories twice, and was just getting edgy about getting in to see Bernie Jacobs when his door opened and out came Diana Dean. She was wearing dark glasses, a short summer dress and the highest heels Charlie had seen since the Victoria Park Carnival. Brian dipped at the knees, and Charlie stood, straight off wishing he hadn't. It was down to envy, probably, because Diana Dean was right at the top of his mother's tree.

'Bye, Bernie.'

'Bye, Di. I'll see you at the O2.'

Brian scurried round from behind his desk to see

the star through the outer doors, and came back with a smugly happy look, his face held still but his nostrils smiling. He arranged and rearranged papers on his desk, and with his top-favour look at Charlie, got up, knocked on Bernie Jacobs' door and went inside. Within seconds, and thank God – because Charlie needed to get out to Debden – the door opened and Bernie Jacobs came out. Tall, with crinkly grey hair, he had the staring eyes of Charlie's form tutor, who was getting used to contact lenses. Already, he was taking off his suit jacket.

'Charlie, come inside.'

Charlie walked into a faint fragrance of Diana Dean.

'"Charisma",' Jacobs said, 'the name of the scent.' He spoke careful Cockney. 'What can we do for our Sally?'

Charlie told him, without giving too much away. The last thing he wanted was for the agency to start thinking his mother was too ill to consider bookings for next year. Charlie desperately wanted next year to be a new life. 'They think it might be good for her and Ron to meet up and chat…'

'So you want to be in touch with Ron? Well, Charlie, I tell you, even Ron's not in touch with Ron. The last time I spoke to him was the morning of Sol Newman's bomb.'

Charlie sat on the edge of the sofa. 'My mother's

only got a phone number and his email, but neither of them are answering. And she can't remember his postal address.'

'You can't ring or email him, anyway. Don't you know?'

'Know what?'

'What happened that night?'

'No.' Charlie's stomach rolled. What was Jacobs going to say?

'Sol told me. I thought he'd have told Stevie...'

'*What?*'

'The bomb goes up. You all go out through the kitchens, is that right? You, Stevie, Sally...'

'Yes, us, and the rest of the audience – '

'But not Ron Moreton. You went home, Sally in a state of shock, but when Sol checked back in the club, Ron was still in there, lying along the piano keyboard, holding his chest.' Bernie Jacobs clutched dramatically at his own breast.

'Shit!'

'So Ron went off in an ambulance to the hospital. And that's the last I've heard from him. But we haven't pursued it, Fliss is probably in a state, she's not been in touch and letters don't get answered. There'll be time enough at the end of the financial quarter. I shouldn't think he's died, though, there'd have been obituaries, and I've have been one of the first to be asked. Or he's getting better, and she's shut him away from any stresses and strains.'

Charlie felt the dropping sensation that hits with a worse-than-bad exam result. From the way his dad had talked, he'd thought Ron had got out OK; this was terrible news. Terrible for Ron himself – and terrible for the chances of being in touch with him. This was going to burn his mother.

'Don't the hospital know how he is?'

'Brian rang, but he's not blood.' Bernie Jacobs shrugged.

'Which hospital was it?'

'The Trafalgar. I think.'

He thinks! 'Ah.' Charlie sat still, looking up at the agent. Fifteen per cent of nothing was nothing, whether it was Sally Julien's nothing, or Ron Moreton's nothing. Bernie Jacobs was already cutting his losses on worry-beads. 'Have you got Ron's home address?'

'Of course. And if you get hold of chapter and verse on him be sure to get word to Brian.' The agent went to his computer and called up the page. 'Got you. Seventeen, Worthing Road, CR10 6EY.' He checked that he'd got it right, tore off a Post-it and wrote on it.

'CR10? Where's that postcode?' Charlie asked.

'Sorry, thought you knew. Croydon. Surrey. Masquerades as part of London.'

Croydon! So that's where he'd got Croydon from, when he was fooling Maevy-baby. Of course Croydon: it was where his mother sometimes went to run through songs with her favourite accompanist.

Bernie Jacobs handed him the note, on which he'd added *Trafalgar Hospital?* Charlie didn't hang around after that, closing his ears to Bernie Jacobs and Brian sending their best love to 'darling Sally'. And all he saw as he walked along Denmark Street was Ron Moreton's head bent over his keyboard, concentrating, his eyes closed, playing his interlude improvisations – great, great piano jazz from a man who had once accompanied Tony Bennett in London – an image that led to another churn in Charlie's stomach. That obscene bomb at Sol Newman's had done more than damage minds and bodies, it could well have robbed the music world of two of its top talents.

9

The black limousine with diplomatic plates drove into the entrance of the Home Office in Marsham Street. On the Power's orders Travonia's ambassador to Britain was making his contact with Home Secretary Jo Baker more formal – 'on the record' this time.

She didn't keep him waiting. Erik Bergovic was taken straight up to her office, and as he entered she was already coming round from behind her desk.

'Do sit down, Ambassador.' They sat opposite each other in hard upholstered armchairs.

'Mr Bergovic…'

'Madam Home Secretary, you will know why I have come.'

'I do, indeed. We haven't caught your suspected dissidents yet, and you wish to know why.' Her words today were tailored for the official recording machine.

Ambassador Bergovic sat up straight. 'We fear a big incident on Travonian soil. There is a celebratory concert to be held in the Dynamo Naraiova Stadium on the sixth of May, where the Chinese trade leadership will be guests of honour – and while we are taking all security precautions, we are still concerned about the possibility of an attack. It's a credible threat to damage the Power and would be very high profile.'

'What sort of attack do you fear?'

'We're picking up chatter about a large explosive device, possibly a vehicle bomb, or something planted in the stadium – although a thorough search will be made. Heavy security will be in place, but we must not alarm the Chinese.'

'That wouldn't do – but in our experience they don't frighten easily. You think such an attack is being masterminded here in London, have I got that right?'

'Certainly. As you know, the Neo-Vlach leader is Zanko Boev, "the Archbishop", and as we speak he is free in your capital.'

There was a pause while coffee was served by her aide, with Jo Baker's favourite ginger-nut biscuits, known for testing diplomatic teeth.

'If Boev succeeds with an atrocity in Travonia,' the ambassador went on, 'will your government disown him when he sets himself up as a regional leader?'

'I can't say at present, that's outside my brief – although our PM is never keen to interfere in other nations' internal affairs. But Boev and his extremist right only want the south, don't they? A new Neo-Vlach state?'

'I say "regional leader", but it's a first step only, Home Secretary, a first step only. It's his moral justification for removing the Power – returning the south to its Orthodox past – but he wants the whole country, believe me, he wants the whole country.'

Jo Baker bit on her biscuit; all her teeth were her own. 'Well, the news is good for you.' She turned, and a briefing sheet was handed to her. 'Our listening people are onto the case as I promised, and the whereabouts of Boev and his conspirators has been narrowed to one London postal code district.' She picked a crumb from out of her blouse. 'How about that?'

Ambassador Bergovic made a move for the pen in his inside pocket.

'A district, of course, that I'm not at liberty to identify.'

He cocked his head.

She leant forward and put a hand on his knee. 'We're going to get them before you do, Erik!'

'I'm very relieved at this progress, Home Secretary. Time is of the essence. If Boev is captured very soon, the Neo-Vlachs will have no credible leader, and the rest of them will run around like headless chickens.'

'I'm pleased to say I've never seen one of those, but I doubt very much that I'd die laughing.' She stood up.

Bergovic followed.

'All ports and airports are on high alert, Ambassador, so I can assure you that Boev won't be able to leave the country to operate from overseas. We've as good as pinned him down.'

'Excellent, Home Secretary.'

Jo Baker signalled for the recording machine to be switched off. 'Would you like a biscuit for the car, Erik?'

He smiled. 'No, thank you. But a crumb of information would be very acceptable.'

She shook her head. 'No way, José. No way. You just have to trust us.'

'Which my government does, of course.' Bergovic gave her a diplomatic bow. 'Thank you for seeing me.'

'My pleasure.' She gave him a now-off-you-go look.

And off he went, with a certain reassurance in his step.

Jo Baker took another ginger-nut for herself. 'Tell GCHQ to just find Boev, quick!' she said, picking crumbs from her blouse again.

Charlie's mother was quiet that night, dressed and sitting out in her chair like a visitor to someone else. And 'visitor' was the word. One of the things that choked Charlie up about this place was the way it was called a care *home* while it was a million miles from being a home. People were here as long as their money lasted, but they were 'guests', 'patients', 'the clientele'; he couldn't remember his mother being referred to as a 'resident' very often. Now she was sitting here looking the way she did on college open evenings, in someone else's world.

Charlie kissed her and opened the window the fifteen centimetres allowed. He checked that his dad had rung, and told her that the Groans sent their love. She nodded and patted the back of his hand, and then she asked her question.

'What about Ronnie?'

Charlie had been going over an answer to that, working out a few words to give her hope instead of bringing her down with the real news of Ron Morton's condition. He put on an upbeat voice. 'I've been to see Bernie Jacobs, and he's given me Ron's address. Although he says he has gone a bit quiet lately.'

'But can you get to him?' Her words came out as if she was casually asking him the time; then her hand suddenly shot out to grip his wrist, hard, almost hurting. 'Prince, I need to see Ron Moreton.'

'As soon as, Mum, as soon as.' And Charlie found himself speechless. There was too much that he dare not say.

She loosened her grip and patted him, sat back. 'It's

good about you and the Bow band.' He'd forgotten that he'd told her about the audition.

She had changed tack, which was good, more like the old Mum. And wasn't thinking about him instead of herself a bit of a move in the right direction? 'And you'll be there, you'll definitely be there for my first gig.'

There was a tap at the door. Charlie got up to open it, but the visitor came in, anyway. It was Dr Leigh, a shortish woman with dark, thick hair and cherry-red lips.

'Bridget told me you were here,' she said to Charlie. 'I think it best I should come to fill you in on some things.' She was foreign – Bridget said Egyptian, married to an English surgeon.

Charlie wasn't sure whether he should stay in here or go outside to hear what the doctor had to say, but she seemed to believe in everything being out in the open because she took the chair he offered and sat down. 'So how do you find your mother today?'

Charlie perched on the bed. 'All right. Better than last Monday, aren't you, Mum?' She looked uncertain about that. He put an arm around her.

'Uh, huh – and have you seen any difference since I adjusted the balance of tablet and talk?' Her words were all cut off at the ends, staccato and strong.

'I think so.' This was difficult for Charlie, discussing his mother while she was sitting there, as if she was one of the Alzheimer patients he'd seen downstairs.

'How do *you* feel, Sally?' Doctor Leigh asked, smiling. 'Better, or worse?'

Sally shrugged.

'We have to do first things first.' She came back to Charlie. 'We have been going through events and memories, and I think we know what we don't know.' Dr Leigh crossed her legs at the ankles, and opened her hands. 'We know about the bomb, and about you, and about your father, and about Mr Newman, and about some other people at the jazz club – and we know about after the bomb, and going home to your flat, and not being able to hear anything for hours. All that is normal, of course.'

Charlie said nothing. *If normal is like living in a world of silent screams!*

'As well as the talking, we have also listened to Sally's music and heard some jazz piano…'

That would be Ron Moreton. So that was how Ron Moreton's name came out…

'Ronnie Moreton,' his mother said.

Charlie had to hold his breath to stop himself from blurting out what he knew about the pianist; Dr Leigh was the sort of forceful and intense person you trusted and wanted to please. Searching for something to say, he came out with, 'Actually, I'm trying to get to see Ron.' But he didn't want her to know that he'd got Ron Moreton's address; he wasn't going to let things race ahead, such as Dr Leigh contacting the Croydon Health Authority before he could get to Ron – it had got to be him.

'Are you happy with this?' Dr Leigh looked across at her patient. 'For your son to make contact with Mr Moreton?'

Sally frowned at the psychiatrist, and then at Charlie, as if the question made no sense. 'Yes,' she said.

'It's pleasing to you that Charlie should see him?'

Now Charlie frowned, too. Was Dr Leigh saying he might find out something that would be too private for him to know? Well if so, the doctor didn't know his mother the way he did, and she didn't know the Ron Moreton he'd met at gigs. Whatever there was to dig out of Sally Julien the soul singer's mind, it wasn't anything shameful, he was totally sure of that.

'Well, that's very good.' Dr Leigh took a card from a small crocodile-skin handbag and gave it to Charlie. 'My number is here. When you have talked to Mr Moreton, will you please tell me anything he remembers of the night?' She smiled at her patient. 'That's going to help us, isn't it?'

'Yes.' But Charlie's mother's eyes said more than that, staring caution at him the way she would when signalling a secret on Stevie's birthday.

Seeing that look, Charlie knew Ron Moreton was the key to something very important. He was surer than ever that finding the man alive would help his mother to improve – and a sudden flood of impatience almost carried him out of that door to get started right now on his search. He desperately needed to find out whatever there was to know about the old jazz pianist, and what had happened between him and his mother. And he was determined to be the one to know it first – because he was family, and that was how families worked, wasn't it?

Tuesday morning's Gravesend to Charing Cross South-Eastern train arrived to a packed platform, the seven-thirty regulars waiting in knots where they knew the doors would stop. Among them was Stefan Remes, dressed in casual gear – a pink open-necked shirt with a black linen jacket, jeans and trainers. But as the doors opened, he didn't move forward. A man behind him had just tapped him on the shoulder, and told him quietly in his own language, 'Take the next train.'

Remes did as he was told. It was no problem to miss this one, the carriages were stuffed, and there were other commuters who couldn't get onto it. He slid back through them and sat on the nearest platform seat, where the man who had spoken to him was reading *The Times*.

'What?' Remes asked.

'I heard in the embassy,' the other man said. 'The ambassador has been told that British Intelligence is close to locating the Archbishop. It's narrowed down to one London postal district.'

'Have they got the postcode?'

'Not yet, but they think it won't be long.'

Remes looked up at the morning sky with its early summer clouds. 'Thanks,' he said. 'He's getting ready for a move, anyway. I'll have to hurry it up.' He swore. 'It's not easy finding somewhere as secret as it needs to be.'

'I thought you should know…'

'You're right. I should. I said thank you. You'll be looked after when…'

'I'll take the next slow train.' The junior Travonian diplomat folded his copy of *The Times* and walked forward on the platform. Remes looked at his watch, and went into the station café and bought a coffee. The next fast train would be in twenty minutes. He would make sure he shouldered his way onto that.

It was past six o'clock by the time Charlie got to Worthing Road in Croydon. But number seventeen was definitely 'shut up and gone away', as Nan Groan would say. The downstairs curtains were open just a crack, and upstairs the blinds were over halfway down. It was the way Stevie had left Mile End Towers when he'd set off for the Travonia tour. The porch was dusty, with a spider's web across a corner, and the grass in the front garden was long. Charlie knocked, and he rang, and he tried the side gate, but it was locked. There was no sense at all of anyone being in the house.

He had already telephoned the Trafalgar Hospital and found out that Ronald Moreton was not on the patient list. He had then phoned Bridget, to tell his mother he wouldn't be coming out to Debden that night – feeling all right about that, because he was on her case. Now he was standing in the front garden of Ron Moreton's house. He thought of Bernie Jacobs' shock news – Sol Newman finding the man clutching his chest – and he thought about Ron Moreton's age. It must have been a heart attack, which could easily have killed him – and now his wife Fliss had shut up the house and moved away…

'Hello? Can I help you?' A woman was calling from next door's front garden. 'She's cancelled the *Advertiser*.'

'Eh? No, I'm not delivering.'

'Can I help you, then?' But she sounded as if that wasn't very likely. She was a smallish woman in a blue housecoat, holding a bright new duster in her hand, and looking at him suspiciously.

'I'm Charlie Peat. My mother's a singer, Sally Julien. Mr Moreton sometimes plays piano with her...'

'Ah.' The woman stopped frowning. 'You know Mr Moreton?'

Know, not *knew*. 'Yes, sort of...'

'Poor Mr Moreton.'

'Why? Is he...? Erm...'

The woman shook her head sadly, coming towards him on her side of the fence. 'I've not seen him. I know he was in hospital, Mrs M. – Felicity – she was off seeing him every day, but she never gave me any bulletins.'

'Only, my mother wants to know any news about him.'

'You say she's a singer?'

'That's right – soul and gospel...She sometimes came here to rehearse.'

'Ah, yes.' The woman put her head to one side, giving him a good looking-over. 'A coloured lady?'

'She's black.'

'I've seen her. Very nice-looking person.'

He guessed this woman saw most of what happened in Worthing Road. But she did seem to trust him. 'Mrs M. gave me an address, just in case. I don't really know why – the postman never delivers, they must be forwarding from the sorting office.' She put her head on one side as if she was making up her mind. 'I'll give it to you, if you like.'

'That'd be great. My mother can...' But the woman was already going back into her house.

He waited; please God the Moretons hadn't gone to relations in Canada, or Australia – that would be the end of the search for him.

The woman came back after two or three minutes. 'Sorry, couldn't find my pencil.' She gave him a sheet of lavender-coloured paper.

He looked at the address. 'East Grinstead,' he read out, 'care of Mrs N. Roberts...'

'I don't know who she is. Could be a sister.'

'Or a daughter,' he offered.

'We weren't close. They kept themselves to themselves.' She lowered her voice. '*She* was a bit of a hippy.'

'Was she? But cheers, thank you very much.'

'You're welcome. Tell your mother to give them both my best – if he's still...' She smiled sympathetically.

'Will do.'

'And shut the gate, won't you? The cats think it's a short cut.'

'Sure.'

He went back to the main road and headed for East Croydon station – beginning to pick at a possible reason for his mother wanting to get hold of Ron Moreton. Without hearing any word from him – no contact, no 'How are you?' – might she think he was mad at her? Sol Newman had interrupted her in the middle of a song, but she'd carried on, and his dad had said, 'The show goes on, Kid.' Could she be blamed for that? Or, getting out through those kitchens, had she looked back and seen Ron slumped at the piano, but done nothing about it? Did she know deep down that he'd been injured in the bomb blast, and she was blaming herself for going on with the show? Was it some sort of guilt that had made her more badly affected than him and his dad, who'd been in the same explosion?

Well, he couldn't know – he wasn't a psychiatrist, and he didn't know if any of that was true – but it could be on the cards, couldn't it? So finding Ron Moreton alive was his best chance of getting to the truth, and given the age of the man, the sooner he did it the better. This was what his secretly living back at home and his lying were all about, why his life had to be more MI5 than Mile End – and something he'd only give up on if he was pinned down and nailed to the floor.

Stefan Remes lived in a quiet cul-de-sac off Singlewell Road in Gravesend. The Victorian house was small – two rooms and a kitchen downstairs, two rooms and a bathroom upstairs. It was joined to another house on one side and separated from its neighbour on the other by a narrow alley, hardly shoulder-wide, but enough in the old days for the coal man to get along to the bunker at the back, and these days for Remes to have an escape route unseen from the porch. Unlike the Tottenham address where Boev and the others were holed up, the residents of Park Road knew one another, they spoke at their cars, and moaned over the fences about slugs and caterpillars. And Remes, in his thirties, always neatly dressed and well spoken, was 'Steve' to his neighbours. Once married to an Englishwoman, Remes hid behind his job as a freelance graphic artist and his weekend photography to work for the cause of his native Travonia with as much explosives on his hands as any other Neo-Vlach. And that night the graphics on which he was working had nothing to do with drawing a diagram of Britain's budget deficit for the *Independent on Sunday*. Up in the back bedroom, under a halogen lamp and through a mounted magnifying lens, he was forging a page to be sewn into a stolen French passport, one of three he'd lifted a few days before from the Eurostar train he'd got off at Ebbsfleet International. Very few people start checking their personal belongings until the Paris train runs into London St Pancras.

Needing total concentration, he had to work in short bursts, and just before seven o'clock he left what he was doing, made himself a strong coffee, and for a change of focal length sat himself in front of the television for Channel Four News. As Zanko Boev's 'British' brain, Remes picked up meanings sometimes hidden inside English talk, and he knew what dull-sounding government statements were really saying. Most important of all, he'd made good contacts with the *Independent*'s writers on Defence and Home Affairs; and it was amazing the sort of screens they left switched on. The news from the night before was always good for starting up a conversation.

He nearly spilt his coffee when 'Travonia' came out of the ether. Will Palmer on Channel Four News was laying out what would be happening on the programme during the next couple of weeks – 'Takes on modern Travonia, and the threat of China's influence in the region.' And they were kicking off straight away with the singer-songwriter Stevie Peat, whose band No Rider was currently touring in the country.

'I spoke to him yesterday in his hotel.'

Without taking his eyes off the television, Remes picked up the remote and started recording, a regular thing when Travonia was on the news. He sat and watched the lean-faced musician with the sensible haircut having a prickly interview with Will Palmer. When it was over, he replayed it. His expression didn't change much, but something he had seen took him back upstairs to his forging of passports with the slightest of smiles.

Dacai was a university town with enough students and young professionals for two No Rider gigs, giving the backline crew a show without a load-out, and another without a load-in. The Sunday off had also been a treat – and very welcome, because this next week was going to be real 'band-on-the-road' stuff, five shows in small towns, taking them back to the north – where, the following week, the tour would climax at the Chinese Celebration Concert in the Dynamo Naraiova Stadium.

'We're doing twenty minutes at the stadium,' Stevie said, 'so we try out a twenty-minute playlist and we open with it at all this week's gigs. We jig things around a bit, settle on the order, and get it solid.'

They were eating their various breakfasts on their way north-west.

'The downside of that would be' – Paul Stoner scooped up runny scrambled egg with his spoon – 'that means at these five gigs we'll be doing all our best stuff first.'

'*All* our stuff's t'rrific,' Nicky mumbled through the nearest thing he'd found to black pudding. 'We gerrit the way it's gonna be – the play-on, the walk-out in blackout, the plug-in, the "one-two-three-four" – an' we hit 'em wi' the opener. No bother.'

Vikki tapped a hard-boiled egg with some precision. 'There will not be blackout, no reveal. Celebration Concert, you play four o'clock in afternoon.'

'Wherever we put the twenty minutes,' Stevie said, 'we settle it today, and we run it all week. Then we'll know when we're swapping guitars, moving in to mics, and what's coming next. We can always reprise a hot number to keep 'em jumping.' That seemed to settle it. 'So what shall we give the Chinese big-wigs? Our bestselling album's *Grassroots*, and it's got "Fervour" on it – always our last encore – so let's close with that. And, working backwards—'

Deano had been quiet over his cornflakes. 'I'll tell you. Open with "Hold Back the Thames", then straight into "Dead Iron Lady". Hit the buggers between the eyes.'

Stevie made notes, and by the time he was on his third coffee the special twenty-minute set had been more or less sorted.

Vikki looked at her watch. 'Splitter call ten minutes. Everyone checked out?'

They were, and their personal bags and instrument cases were in the hotel doorway. Sean O'Hara stood there with Stevie. 'Did you tell your boy to save his old man's TV interview?'

'No, I wasn't proud of it, mate, because I'm not proud we're doing the Celebration Concert. Will Palmer was right about integrity; kid ourselves if we like, we are definitely selling our souls to the devil.'

'Even if you reckon you are, bucko, it's for a top o' the tree reason. Think of what it's doing for your Sally…'

Vikki clicked her organiser bag shut and went through to the lobby.

'Anyhow, I need to text Charlie.' Stevie looked thoughtful. 'Give him your congrats on his first job. I'd hoped he'd send me a bit more on how it went…'

'He's a good kid. An' good kids are busy little sparks. He's just living his own life – the same as you an' me. Why don't you take your own medicine, man. Bit of therapy. Get settled in the van an' write a new song. You'll feel all the brighter for that.'

'I wish I could,' Stevie said as the splitter pulled up and he shouldered his two guitars. 'I bloody wish I could.'

Zanko Boev and Stefan Remes had regular rendezvous, each one set up at the previous meeting, so that telephone contact could be cut down; but this had been arranged as a priority. It was in Tottenham Court Road, where the pair of them were looking at the window of an electronics shop. It was a chilly early summer afternoon and Boev was wearing a silk scarf up round his face and his woollen hat pulled down over his ears. Remes was in a smart black raincoat, a leather satchel slung over his shoulder – just like anyone on their way home from work who was looking out for a bargain gadget.

Neither looked at the other. They hadn't come to the shop window together, and they wouldn't leave it at the same time. The traffic surged up Tottenham Court Road from the Oxford Street lights, and even a close passerby wouldn't have known whether or not they spoke to one another. But after a lengthy perusal of the window display they went their separate ways, first one, and, three minutes later, the other: Remes south towards the tube, and Boev north towards a bus stop. And no one in the world would have taken the least bit of notice of the rendezvous, let alone have any idea of the arrangements the two terrorists had just made.

10

Charlie got through to Bridget on her mobile phone.

'It's Charlie Peat.'

This call was crucial. If his mother had gone backwards he'd see her tonight. But if Bridget reckoned she was OK he'd phone her instead, and let her know he was off to look for Ron Moreton, down in Sussex. He wouldn't let her down.

'How are you today, Charlie? Growing tall in this persistent rain?'

'OK. I'm in the dry right now.'

'An' that's where you want to stay, my boy. It's coming down on Debden like Noah's flood.'

'I'm just calling about Mum. How's she doing today?'

'Keeping out of the wet stuff for a start, played your da's CD after her lunch.'

That gave Charlie a lift. He wasn't exactly having the best day of his life. He'd just been warned of dire consequences if he didn't get his history coursework in by Friday – although what were AS grades compared with what he'd got to do? And Bijan had gone on about seeing Stevie on the news when Charlie hadn't – and that had opened up a whole new can of worms. *What if the Groans had seen the interview? Or someone at church had told them about it?* What if they realised Stevie was still touring in Travonia, and their Charles was lying his head off? His only hope was that they were at their regular Bible class when it was on – and that no one else had blabbed.

'I'll give Mum a ring,' he told Bridget.

'Don't be bothering with that – I'm walking her corridor this minute. Hold on…' Charlie heard the knocking on the door, and, 'Sally, love, I've got a handsome devil of a young man to speak to you here. Would you be in for a call from a certain Charlie Peat?'

And his mother was. 'Hello, Charlie.' Her voice wasn't as bright as he'd hoped – but who could beat Bridget at bright? 'Have you found Ron?' Straight to it, like a kid.

'That's what I'm on to tonight, Mum, instead of coming to see you. Following up a lead. Is that OK?'

'Yes.' Said very straight.

'But I'll be in touch as soon as.'

'Yes.' Straight again. 'You find Ronnie for me.'

'I'll do my best, you bet. Cheers, Mum. Tons of love.'

'I'll give you back to Bridget.'

It seemed like one step forward and two steps back; and no 'Prince' today.

'Love you.'

'Yes.'

Bridget came on again. 'Oh, and we heard about your da brightening up the TV screen. Proud as punch, we were, weren't we, Sally?'

'I didn't see it myself, Bridget, but...Listen, I've got to go.'

'Good luck to you, Charlie.'

Within seconds of ending the call Charlie was rooting out a hooded waterproof. Grove Road, like the rest of the South East, was deluged by rain. It bounced up off the streets and ran in great drops down the windowpanes. But, fine weather or foul, that talk with his mother made Charlie want to get out to East Grinstead pronto. She might be a bit better than she'd been last week, but she definitely needed some word about Ron Moreton or she'd soon be back on the yawning tablets.

The front room of the Tottenham house had been cleared of religious paraphernalia, which was all packed with the bags and hard cases of electronic gear that were cluttering the hall. Upstairs, Tomescu was cleaning surfaces with anti-bacterial wipes, while downstairs Stoica was organising the quick pick-ups into pairs, left hand, right hand; Zanko Boev was keeping watch through the slats of the front-room blinds.

'The vans haven't moved. One at each end of the street. No one gets into them, no one gets out of them.'

'Well, we know who's sitting inside – and it's not gas fitters.' Stoica left his organising to look out through the slats himself. 'It's not the rain. They're waiting for us to make a move. Fifty houses in this road, we've kept cell-net silence, so they're waiting for us to show ourselves.'

'Tell Tomescu to leave the wiping,' Boev instructed. 'It's unnecessary. They know who's here. Get back to the hallway and divide the necessary from the unnecessary. Take only the cross of the Lord, the phones and the computers, whatever the three of us can carry in one run. We're moving to the new place fast.'

'It would be to the airport if the fat man had done his money-raising properly. The passports are ready, we know where we're picking them up...'

Boev didn't leave the slats. 'That may be – but no final payment, no attack.'

'How short are we?' Stoica was already out in the hall.

'Three thousand euros. Call up to Tomescu. Tell him we're getting out now.'

Stoica shouted up for Tomescu to get his fat arse down the stairs.

Boev came out to the hall. 'If there's trouble, sacrifice yourself, sacrifice Tomescu – but in the name of the Lord I've got to stay free to sign the bank transfer.'

Stoica patted the Makarov nine-millimetre pistol in his pocket. 'You'll get away.' He shouted at Tomescu. 'And you tie up your laces in case you have to run.'

'I hate running –'

'Then waddle, as usual.'

'I mean I hate skulking from place to place this way. I'm a soldier for the Neo-Vlachs and for Christ the Lord. I want to be standing up and fighting the enemy...'

'Not with those feet of yours.'

'Get on with it!' Boev shouted, back in the front room. 'We've got to move fast, before they kick in through the windows.'

Stoica checked through the slats, too. 'Both gas vans are facing the same way...'

'So in five minutes we make the call.' Boev pulled out a new and unused pay-as-you-go phone and gave it to Stoica. 'Tell Remes to bring in the transport from the east end of the road, then those vans have to turn around to chase us...'

Out in the hall the essential cases and bags were set to go.

'Ready,' said Boev, still eyeing the street. 'Make the call.'

Stoica tapped in the number, which rang another new mobile phone in a mocked-up Electricity Company Transit just around the corner. The 'get out' was on.

Charlie had travelled enough with Stevie and Sally to know that a musician doesn't live a Ritz Hotel life. Sound checks with stroppy engineers, lavatory-like dressing rooms, eating at midnight, van calls at one in the morning; 'the road' was tough. But how much worse to be on a rush-hour train in and out of London every weekday of your life! Pressed against a partition with a fat Sweatball shouting through his mobile into his face, the train windows steamed up in the soggy air, to Charlie it was like a bad film where throwaway newspapers were the props, loud mobiles were the soundtrack, and the plot was, could he grab a seat before he got to East Grinstead?

The route to Esseherst Road was on his BlackBerry, as well as the information that he'd need a 291 bus to take him to the Three Crowns at Ashurst Wood.

And, *yes!* He beat Sweatball to a seat at Oxted, but he'd hardly finished a finger-face on the window when the train pulled into East Grinstead station, and he swished in his waterproof to the doors. The driver of the 291 Metrobus promised to give him good notice for getting off at the Three Crowns, and for a few minutes he sat and relaxed, took in some deep breaths, and unfocused his eyes. And it could have been something about the rhythm of the bus that lulled Charlie for a while – but he found himself in one of those might-have-been wanderings that come before sleep; about Francine.

Wouldn't it have been great if he'd told her his secret early on? He'd been stupid not to let her know what he was up to. He trusted her, he really liked her, and he reckoned he was a bit special to her. She'd rooted for him over the Rubber Girders and spoken up for him when he hadn't showed – and on the night of the audition she'd kissed him and they'd held hands all the way back. So why hadn't he brought her in on things? His stomach flipped when he thought about her; even in the grind of college a wink from Francine could light up a boring lesson. And right now, tucked in next to him in another squelching waterproof, how great it would have been if she'd been with him on this mission to find Ron Moreton…

'Three Crowns!' The bus driver brought Charlie back to where he was.

'Cheers.'

The rain had stopped now, and with Google maps he soon found his way to the address the Croydon neighbour had given him.

Number 129 had a fifty-metre gravel drive leading up to the house. Under dark, dripping trees it seemed to exist in a world of its own, and as Charlie walked further from the road he half expected a guard dog to come running at him. But the house at the top had a window facing down the drive, and by the time Charlie got to the front door it was half open, with a defensive-looking woman peering round the woodwork.

'Can I help you?'

'Are you Mrs Roberts?'

'I am.' The woman opened the door a fraction wider. She was tall, holding herself straight, with grey hair swept up on top.

'A neighbour of Mr and Mrs Moreton in Croydon gave me your address.'

'Oh, really? Mrs Pearce? That was for random deliveries.'

No way was Charlie going to be inferior to some delivery, so he came straight out with it. 'Ron Moreton plays with my mother. Sally Julien, the singer. She's asked me to try to find him.'

Mrs Roberts suddenly smiled. 'Ron Moreton's my father...'

And she didn't say 'was'.

'Come in, will you? Take off your cagoule out there, and come into the dry. What's your name?'

'Charlie. Charlie Peat.'

'Come in, then, Charlie. I'm Nancy.'

He hung his waterproof next to others in the porch, wiped his feet carefully, and stepped into the house.

Nancy Roberts lowered her voice. 'I'll just warn you about Dad,' she said gravely. 'And get you a drink. What would you like, grape juice? Red or white?'

'Red, please.'

She ushered him into an empty sitting room, waved at an old armchair. 'I won't be a tick.' And she shut the door on him.

—Leaving Charlie to sit fretting over what she was going to warn him about Ron Moreton. After getting this far, was everything about to come crashing down? Was he going to discover why that feeling of dread had been gnawing at him?

They were terrorist killers ready to shoot their way out of the hole-up – but what they didn't know was that the two gas vans weren't packed with Special Unit officers but with members of the MI5 surveillance team pinpointing phone signals, two thirds of a triangulation – with the third vehicle round the corner. And just now they'd picked up a 'virgin' blip from a new phone, the strong local signal they were listening for. Immediately, the security people were deciphering the phone's message, while GCHQ sat-navs were doing the fix before the anti-terrorist squad was sent in. Screens were searched, earphones turned up, and not enough notice was taken of a London Electricity Board van coming along the street.

It was close, all the same. Even as Boev ran across the pavement and climbed into the transit, the triangulation was done, and MI5 had their fix.

'Number fifty-five, on the north side.'

And from T-Mobile – 'Voice message. Accented. Could be Travonian – we're getting a translation.'

The message went to the attack squad waiting around the corner. 'Call up the cavalry!'

'Direct them, then. Which one's fifty-five?'

'Right-hand side. Fifty-one, fifty-three, fifty-five! By that LEB transit.'

'Bugger! Go! Go! Go!'

But the electricity van had sped off; by the time the British Gas vans had done their five-point turns, Boev and the others were heading down the A10, ready for a swap with yet another mocked-up van – provided by Remes' scrapyard compatriots from Ruxley Corner, north Kent – with prayers to the Lord being offered up in its cab.

11

Nancy Roberts came into her sitting room carrying Charlie's glass of grape juice.

'Just a quick word first about Pops,' she said.

Charlie took the glass, but he couldn't sip, not yet. What was she going to say – that Ron Moreton would be angry for what his mother had done, going on with the show after the bomb warning? That her dad had gone ga-ga, and there wouldn't be any sense got out of him?

'Don't take him as you see him,' Nancy Roberts warned. 'He won't look the sharp jazz pianist you saw last time. He won't fix you with any spell. But please bear in mind, Charlie – he's still Ron Moreton inside.'

Charlie waited for her to say some more, that feeling of dread still with him. But she didn't, she stood there offering him a hand up. Thank God for that; she was just protecting her father from any shocked looks.

'Bring your drink with you, Charlie,' she said as she took him into the next room off the hall.

The first thing he saw was the polished grand piano, its top down, the next was Ron Moreton in a wheelchair, sitting by a window overlooking a long garden. Or it could have been Ron Moreton's father – Nancy had been right to warn him, although he remembered Ron as an old man, anyway, with a bald head and horn-rimmed glasses, but still a sharp, clean-shaven jazz virtuoso, leaning over his keyboard and playing the best piano ever, young in his own way like most top musicians. This Ron Moreton had no glasses, his eyes were in deep sockets, and an old man's wispy beard blurred the outline of his face. Sitting next to him, holding a mug with a straw to his lips, was Fliss, dressed in a Keswick Jazz Festival T-shirt and shorts. Charlie hadn't been able to recall her face, but seeing her now, he knew who she was.

'He likes his tea. No matter how cold it gets, he won't leave it till he's made a disgusting sucking noise at the end.'

Ron Moreton pulled his mouth away from the straw. 'That's what…we all do…when we go,' he said in a trembly, hard-to-catch voice.

'What's that, Ronnie?'

'Make a disgusting sucking noise.'

'See what I mean?' Nancy said. 'He's the same old curmudgeon underneath.'

Fliss offered the straw again. 'Just make sure you don't pop off while I'm around.'

'Try not to.' Instead of managing a wink Ron stared through his hollow eyes at Charlie.

'This is Sally's son,' Nancy said, taking Charlie over to the wheelchair, and relieving him of his glass.

'I...know it is.'

'Sit your bum down here.' Fliss got up. 'Ronnie's very pleased to see you.'

'I can...tell him that,' Ron mumbled. 'Both speak English...don't need...translators.' He waved a bony arm at Charlie.

That rotten bomb! Charlie thought – his mother in a care home, and Ron Moreton unable to hold a cup to his lips, let alone lift his piano lid.

Charlie sat down, turning the chair so he was face to face with the man. 'Mum asked me to try to see you.'

Ron stared at him for a long while. 'How...is...she?' He leant forward, breathing loudly. 'Angry. Uh?... Angry? *Wild?*'

'No.' Charlie shook his head. 'Upset. Not angry...'

'Upset, then...with me...?' The old man was trying to lift himself from his wheelchair to get closer, his hands like white claws on its arms.

'No, she's not angry with you, or upset, or anything.' Charlie couldn't see where this was going. 'It's more like the other way round.'

Ron closed his eyes; his hands trembling in his agitation.

'Ronnie, man...' Fliss was distressed.

Charlie had seen his mother frustrated like this, and he wanted to calm things. He thought for a second or two – and then he came out with it; it was something that could all be in his head, but he'd been growing more and more certain about it over the past few days.

'I think Mum thinks you blame her for staying on stage after the bomb warning...Some stupid "show must go on" tradition.'

His words fell into a weird silence – until Fliss broke it.

'Well, I'll be jiggered.'

Ron was shaking his head, slowly and deliberately.

'Ronnie's been thinking the same funky thing...' Fliss put a hand on Charlie's shoulder. 'This silly old goat has got it into his *tête* that Sal hasn't been to see him because *she's* wild with *him*...'

'No.' Charlie turned to her. 'She thinks *he's* cross with *her*. But she couldn't come to tell you because...I don't know if you've heard...but she's ill, she's in Stage Left getting help...'

Fliss did a little shriek. 'Stage Left? God! Oh, no. What a downer! Poor Sal. That explains it, doesn't it, Ronnie?' Her face suddenly looked years younger, like her clothes. 'You give her buckets of love from us.' She kissed Charlie, for passing on to Sally. 'It's exactly the same with Duke Ellington here – he had a heart attack, and then a stroke, so he couldn't go anywhere either.' She turned to Ron. 'Ronnie, it's like a silly-arse farce. Each of us thought the other one was in a huff…'

Charlie could hardly believe what he'd heard: Ron Moreton hadn't been angry with his mother, he'd thought she was wild with him. *Hallelujah!* like the Groans would say. This was just what she needed to hear.

Now Nancy cut in. 'I don't know if your mother knew at the time – Pop's a secretive old fox where his career's concerned – but he had a BBC producer in Sol Newman's that night, someone in charge of a big jazz broadcast in the summer…'

'You'll know what it meant to him, Charlie,' Fliss took it up. 'A George Shearing birthday tribute going out in August. Instead of coming straight off at the break, Ronnie was going to give them "Lullaby of Birdland" as a sort of audition piece. Huh! Should a musician like Ronnie have to do an audition piece for some tin-pot BBC producer aged twelve?'

'No way! Totally, no way.' Charlie was starting to feel light in the head. So, like his mother, Ron Moreton hadn't wanted to stop the show. He looked round at Fliss and Nancy. 'It was the same with Mum. Sol Newman books artists he might have on his TV show. She wanted to give him the works that night.'

Fliss half throttled him with two arms round his neck. 'Charlie – it's so groovy you found us! Took the trouble to go to Worthing Road and to come out here...' She half throttled again.

'I had to. For Mum.' He just about choked it out.

But Ron Moreton was looking a long way from delighted. He was groaning, and stretching in his wheelchair, his face twisted in frustration. He shook his head fiercely. 'For me – not just...Shearing's tribute. Not only.'

'We know, Ronnie. Don't—'

'Hear...me!' He flicked a hand at Fliss, not taking his socket eyes off Charlie. 'When...I was a child...my mother...sneaked me out of Germany. From the Nazis. She sent me...from Berlin, to America.'

'We know, Ronnie – the "One Thousand Children". Charlie doesn't want to hear all that.'

'She...stayed behind. A Jew.' Ron Moreton swiped a backhand at the wiping-out of his mother. 'I have never...ever again...run away from evil.'

'Pops!'

Ron cleared his throat with a loud bark. 'Sol said…
"suspect car". Our…choice. Stay or…go. Run! This is…
what all fanatics want. Fear.' He lifted his bony arm to
wipe spittle from his lips. 'And I would not…run in fear.'

'No, Ronnie, love.'

Charlie couldn't think of anything to say – he wanted
to hug this old pro who'd also been dead set against
leaving that stage, too; because if his mother's problem
was to do with guilt, this put her in the clear, didn't it?
She could not be blamed for Ron Moreton's heart attack.

'I warned you about Pops,' Nancy said. 'The piano
frustrates him, so we have his tirades instead.'

'Huh!' said Fliss. 'I've always had his tirades.' She put
an arm around her husband's shoulders. 'And I wouldn't
do without 'em for all the pot in Potsdam.'

Charlie stood up. With what he'd just heard he
wanted to get back to the flat to do some coursework,
to get something in for Friday – and then take himself
out to Debden the next evening. His mother had got to
hear this news asap. Who knew – it could be the start of
a proper recovery…

But Ron Moreton hadn't finished. 'Bring…Sal to see
me…when she's ready,' he said. 'Or I'll…get my bike
out…and come to see her.' He looked so deadly serious
that Charlie half believed he'd do it. 'We'll…perform!'

And he put on a brave, lit-up musician's face that Charlie wouldn't get out of his head all the way home. He accepted Nancy's offer of a lift to East Grinstead station. And, after a long, gripping shake of the hand from Ron, which had almost as much feeling in it as the great old pianist's words, he hurried out to the car.

'And love to dear Sal,' Fliss called after him. 'We'll leave her in peace till she's ready – but the world can't afford to shut away a voice like hers in Stage Left.'

'Dead right!'

Delighted with his visit, Charlie imagined his mother's face when he told her Ron Moreton's brilliant news. He could hardly wait; but it was too important for texting. First of all, though, when he got indoors, he'd gather his thoughts and send an upbeat message to Stevie.

In that frame of mine he headed home on 'automatic', his head all over the place with what he now knew; definitely in too much of a haze when he got there to notice the marks on the paintwork of the street door that stood between him and his laptop.

But as he let himself into the Grove Road flat his body froze at what he saw coming at him, and no way could he know what suddenly hit him from behind.

*　*　*

The concert venue at Posti was top flight. The sound check was professional, the dressing room was clean, and the rider had been met to the letter. The band might be called No Rider but Vikki made sure its contract rider was always met to the full – or there wouldn't be a gig. The rider laid down the technical needs of the band, and all the other necessities such as towels, soap, and tissues – plus the popular part of the deal: food and drink for band and crew. This was nothing outlandish: beers, wine, Coke (not Pepsi), a bottle of vodka, still water, sandwiches, and a 'buy-out' allowance for food at the hotel. The No Rider musicians weren't like a lot of rock groups; they didn't throw wild backstage parties, and being a long way from home, their personal guest list was zero, unless Deano had invited a local girl. All these requirements were met by Posti's Teatrul Patria. The band didn't carry much lighting – the show was music and words, not smoke and lights – and the Patria's rig was basic but effective. The mixer was up-to-date enough for Winny Beckford; in the sound check he could use the in-ear monitor system with its handy 'talk to stage' channel. Together, everything added up to the prospect of a good night.

The evening opened with a local support band – Mono Boyz – which Vikki held strictly to its forty-minute slot. Then, as dry ice rolled out, on ran No Rider, all in black except Deano jumping up and down in his white frockcoat – going straight into 'Hold Back the Thames' and the twenty-minute Dynamo Stadium set. The audience jumped with them all through the show to the finish and a reprise of 'Fervour' – Stevie and the rest sweating through their shirts, wet fingers slipping and sliding on guitar strings, and Nicky Harris's drumsticks flashing like lightning rods.

'Thank you, Posti!'

Stevie towelled his face and rushed through to the merchandising stand in the foyer, where Vikki was already surrounded by customers.

'Good gig,' she said.

'Yeah – went OK.' Stevie was straight off signing a plastered arm, before getting into the routine of passing CDs and T-shirts around the band. 'Might swap "Headless Rooster" for something else in the stadium set.'

'Why?'

'Something quieter,' Stevie shouted in the clamour, 'where the words can count for more on TV.'

Vikki nodded, and they went on selling and signing until, with a rattling of padlocks and chains, the foyer doors were half closed, ready to see the last punters out – when a woman was suddenly confronting Stevie, shoving a *Dirty Money* CD at his face.

'Where's your credibility now, Stevie Peat?' She was Scottish, and furious.

'Credibility?' The CD she was holding hadn't been sold to her here; it was old, and the case was split. Its cover was a mock-up of the band playing to a roomful of third-world children working at old sewing machines.

'I thought you people stood for something! I've seen you in Glasgow, Aberdeen, London – and I was queen of City Hall when I saw you were going to be out here the same time as me…'

'*But?*'

'Bollocks to "but"!' She said the word as if it had three t's on the end. 'What the hell is your band doing, playing like monkeys for the organ-grinding president of this arse-hole country?'

Security was moving in on her, and O'Hara was tugging at Stevie's arm.

'You don't know what we're going to play,' Stevie said, lamely.

'You can play whatever you like. No one's going to hear what you're singing. But you and your wee friends will still be stood up there performing on state TV for the president of a corrupt capitalist country. I used to have respect for you…' She was being lifted backwards towards the door. 'If you want to know who'll be spitting on your "Spittle Pavement" from now on, it's this one! And you can flush your wit and satire down the lavvie.' She tried to throw the album at Stevie, but the grip on her arm meant it fell to the floor at her own feet, where she kicked it away in disgust.

'Nutter!' said Paul Stoner.

Nicky Harris shrugged. 'Can't please 'em all.'

Vikki patted Stevie's cheek. 'Not worry.'

Stevie picked up the separated pieces of the album and took them to the rubbish bin in the corner, where he dropped them in, one, two, three.

'The wee lassie could be cor-rect,' he said. The others laughed. But his face said that using the worst Scottish accent ever was only a jokey cover-up. For the second time that week he had been rocked back on his heels.

Boev ordered Otto Stoica to drag the boy into the bedroom at the back of the flat.

'Check for life. If he's alive, tie him. Gag him.'

Boev was wearing blue overalls spattered with white paint. Stoica was dressed the same, and lined up inside the front door were tins of Dulux, looking as if East European labourers had come to do the place up while Stevie Peat was away on tour. Also in overalls,

Tomescu was downstairs in the studio, plugged into the Peats' phone line and the internet, his urgent task the completion of the fundraising; but his headphones let through the commotion from above. As quickly as he could, he pulled himself up the stairs to see a boy being dragged into the top bedroom – bleeding from a cut to the back of his head, his mouth open, his limbs limp, and his eyes closed.

'Who the hell is this?'

'You tell me.' Stoica dragged Charlie by the feet, bumping him roughly over the threshhold of the bedroom. 'Remes has cocked up, big time. This place was supposed to be empty…'

'Peat's a white man. This kid's black…'

Boev had joined them. 'Get into his pockets, find his phone, everything will be on that.'

But Stoica was looking at a photograph on the bedroom wall, of a man, a woman, and the boy at someone's wedding – suits, silk dress and hat. 'Look there. He's the son.'

Tomescu went through the boy's pockets, while Stoica ripped the flex from a bedside lamp and tied his ankles together, tight. He pulled the flex from a second lamp and lashed the boy's wrists behind his back, kicking his body over to get them where he wanted.

'Phone,' Tomescu said, finding a BlackBerry and throwing it to Boev. 'There's gaffer tape downstairs.' He pulled himself up from the floor and puffed off down to the studio.

Boev stared at the phone's contacts list. 'Half the world on this.' He scrolled up and down. 'And "Stevie".'

Stoica was wiring the ankle flex to the radiator feed as Tomescu came back with a roll of silver gaffer tape.

'Not the mouth, not yet,' Boev said. 'Leave the door open. If he lives, we'll hear him. We need more information before we kill him. And get Remes here, fast! He checked out this place with his newspaper's music editor. Told Peat's agency he was a Russian booker. The man's in Travonia but the wife's taking time out, so be on stand-by to evacuate through the rear. This is the son – so when does the mother come home, I want to know that.'

'We can kill one, we can kill the other. Easy.' Stoica kicked the boy. 'And we've got a secure landline here, we only need three days if Tomescu's to be believed.'

'I'll get the money!'

Boev fixed Stoica with a hard look. 'See beyond the end of your nose! Where does this boy have to be tomorrow? Who is going to miss him? And when the mother comes back who's she going to meet for shopping or coffee after you've killed her? If there's any suspicion, any mystery, no contact when the father expects it, he'll send the police to come checking.'

Stoica shrugged. 'I've got my Makarov nine mill and silencer – and enough ammunition to fight a war.'

'This place suits us without the stink of death – a live, unmonitored landline. But before we do anything we need information from the boy, urgent. You, Tomescu, get back to the money calls. You, Stoica, forget your Makarov for ten minutes, get to the kitchen and keep a keen eye out at the back – and hope you didn't hit the boy too hard. We need him alive until we find out what we need to know. Then we kill him.'

Stoica smiled. 'And that's my top speciality,' he muttered.

12

Thanks to a special condition attached to the stadium concert contract, Vikki had booked No Rider into a country hotel on the outskirts of the capital, all able to order what they liked and everything paid for. Now it was three days' rest for the band until sound check the day before the concert.

'Me – I don' give a monkey's what anyone says,' Nicky Harris kept saying. 'I could get used to a life of privilege.'

But Stevie was morose. Even basking in the warm sun on the patio, his face said this was one of those times when nothing in the world could lift him. 'Not a word from Charlie for a while,' he told Deano. 'Kid's gone dead quiet.'

'Like you, then.' Deano's sunglasses were up on his forehead as he looked at a lurid magazine. 'Could be his memory's full, or his charger's packed up, or his love life's more important than some miserable old sod of a father spreading gloom and despondency all over the place.'

'Thanks for that.'

'Ring the Groans if you're worried.'

'I'm not worried,' Stevie snapped. 'And they'd only

make him write out "I must text my father" a hundred times. No...'

'I know what's really up –' Deano turned to look at him – 'You're still spooked by Will Palmer and the bollocking you got from Mary Queen of Scots.'

'No, I'm not...'

'Yes, you are – and you know it.' Deano threw down the magazine. 'You're in a bind about gigging for a corrupt government. You reckon you've sold your radical soul down the Swanee...'

Stevie stayed staring across the grass and into the trees. 'Perhaps I'm just not so much agitprop as aged-pop...'

'You ought to be looking at all this through my glasses.' Deano slipped them back onto his nose. 'Polarised. Dead clear. See things they way they are.'

'And that is how...?' Stevie turned his head, but not far enough to meet Deano's eye.

'Well, look at how Sally's in a top nursing home, well cared for, getting the best help money can buy – because doing these gigs and signing up for their gala spectacular is earning us multiple dosh. Ask Vikki, if it's slipped your mind – saying yes to this Chinese thing was the clincher for us getting the tour in the first place, and how it'll be the clincher for getting us an autumn tour and a winter tour, all on top potato. Even the Stones wouldn't have got what we're getting, so all the boys are doing well out of it. And look at the cost – twenty short minutes in the Dynamo Stadium, Friday. So, cheer up, you miserable old sod, because by you doing *your* best thing, the medics can do *their* best thing for Sally…'

But Stevie had gone back to staring into the trees.

'…So now I'm going to tell you what else you're going to do…'

'I thought you might.'

'You wanted to put something quieter in for "Headless Rooster". More meaning to the words, right? Well, why don't you pull out your pen and start writing yourself a new solo.' Deano swivelled round. 'I've got a great tune in my head, and I've got a rhythm I've been keeping for something mondo. So you write something new to console yourself, and take a smack at the president and the Power. Sing a couple of verses of radical words to the VIP seats and then it'll all be hunky. Not too much in their face, make it something subtle. Yes? You can flaunt your socialist conscience while you pocket your capitalist cash.' Deano picked up his magazine again and flapped it noisily to say he was going to keep quiet from now on.

'Perhaps that's the least I could do,' Stevie muttered. 'But I still wish the little tyke would text…'

And when Deano was back into his magazine he put a hand to the pocket where he kept his pen.

Charlie came through a dark mist with his head pounding and his stomach looping. Where was he? What had happened? Had the train crashed? Had a bomb gone off? *Was he dead?* He tried to focus his eyes, but it was as if his head was deep in bubble-wrap; to see anything at all he had to close one eye, and then his insides dived again and he wanted to vomit. He tried to kick out his legs to stop the keeling, but they wouldn't move – and they hurt like hell. He tried to lift himself, but his hands were fixed behind his back, with something sharp cutting into his wrists. He rolled his head – he could just roll his head – and taking in a deep breath to stop himself being sick, he coughed into the carpet.

God – please make this stop! His brain seemed to be pushing out through his eye-sockets and the nausea was throwing his insides around. He just wanted to die. Dying would be good: this terrible pain would go away, this somersaulting would stop, and he wouldn't be choked up with vile vomit. *So unless this was Hell, he couldn't be dead – because Heaven would be so peaceful.* And through one eye, the only way he could hold things still for a second or two, he could see curtains, a wardrobe, a window sill with a wig on a stand, a radiator. More pounding, more twisting, his feet vaulting over his head, his stomach diving to the depths and soaring up. And now with the other eye he could see an open door, a tunnel, and a distant place where someone was standing. He lifted his head and sucked in a great mouthful of air to roar out his distress. But no roar came, just a great groaning, and a spasm of vomit spewing all over the carpet – stomach, blood, bile – and he laid his face back into its hot stink.

But not for long. There was the sound of running and the blur of boots and hands. His head was suddenly yanked up by the hair, something hard thudded into his back, and a punch socked into his cheek.

'Who? Who?' a voice was saying.

He could just see a BlackBerry in front of him; but no way could he read what was thrust at his face. He was held sitting up; beyond the BlackBerry he could see his legs, his trainers, and the tying to the radiator that was holding him down.

'Who?' A boot cracked into his spine again. He shouted in pain, but what came out was more vomit and blood, all over his jeans.

'Give that to me.' This voice sounded more English, where the first had been foreign. But Charlie couldn't see either of these people. He was facing the radiator and the closed curtains at the window – and now he realised where he was. The wig on the window sill was what his mother wore for her Roberta Flack set. This was his parents' bedroom: he was at home, in the flat at Grove Road.

'I will read you a name, and you will tell me who is this person.'

'Who…are…you?' he tried to ask – but it came out as blood and bubble.

'Shuddup!' Another kick cracked into his back. 'This name. "Stevie". This your father?'

They'd been nosing around in the flat. Why get a broken spine over stuff they already knew? 'Yes.' He nodded and his head hurt more.

'Stevie Peat of "No Rider"?'

Gulp. Swallow. '…Yeah…'

'Where is he?'

Who were these men? Burglars? Illegal immigrants? Al Qaeda? Terrorists?

'Travonia? Eh?' *Thwack!* Another vicious punch took him hard round the side of his face, keeling him over, more blood, running from his nose. They yanked his body up, with someone pulling at his hair again and stretching his aching neck. 'Travonia? Uh?'

He couldn't take this any more. He nodded again, and got the word out on bloody dribble. 'Yes.'

'And this "Mum". This is Sally Julien?'

'Yes.'

'Where is she? Right now. This exact moment. Just.'

No, they weren't getting his mother.

'Aunt…funeral…Ireland.'

'That was said very quick.'

This man didn't believe him. Charlie braced himself for the next kick, or punch. He hadn't known what to say. What was safer, that she'd walk in any second, or that she was off the scene? He didn't know – anyhow, he'd said it now. Just so long as they couldn't get to her. He had good news to give his mum.

'She leaves you alone here? A kid?'

The hand had stopped pulling his hair, but he fought not to slump, trying to sit as tall as he could. 'Eighteen… I'm eighteen…Adult…Student. University. I'm allowed.' He heard himself sounding like Ron Morton – and every word a pain.

'"Fran-cine". This text. What does she mean, "Rubber Girders"? Who is this Fran-cine?'

Who is Francine? He tried to draw in a deep breath through his bloody nose. *Francine is someone you will never get your dirty hands on!* He said nothing, waited for the pain that was coming any second. And it had to come, because he would never betray Francine.

Or, would he? When it came, it was ten times worse than anything they'd done to him already. And he saw who did it – a thin-faced man in dirty overalls who came round in front of him, swore at him in some foreign language, ripped open his jeans, tore at his jockeys, and with a hard claw of a hand grabbed his testicles and squeezed and squeezed and twisted – and then punched his ringed fist into them. A searing pain tore up through his body, as if his front and his guts had been ripped out, a sick, hollow convulsion of agony. He would have screamed like a tortured pig if his mouth hadn't been clamped shut by another foul hand. He felt the blood vessels breaking in his eyes, his back arching in a rictus; and a blanket of black as his brain went out on him.

But for seconds only. Too soon he was conscious again, still lying in his own foul mess, and still with the same question being asked.

'This Fran-cine. Who is she?'

And he felt gutted in shame as he fought to overcome

his paralysis and answer the man. 'My…girlfriend.'

'Ah.' He was thrown back like a sack of rubbish, his groin open to the world and vulnerable to whatever they wanted to do next – scared out of his mind at what that would be. But when they told him, he knew he would hate himself more than he hated them.

'You send a text to this Fran-cine, in good normal way for her. She knows it comes from you, genuine.'

'No!' He cowered, waiting. But nothing happened this time; this man's voice just sounded more oily, reasonable.

'Is all you do, and all is OK. You say your father is ill and so you go to be with him. Travonia. Very soon. Bye-bye. Love. Sign the way you sign for her.'

The BlackBerry was put into his left hand, and angled so that his right thumbnail could just touch the keys.

'You do this.'

He couldn't see who was speaking, but the thin-faced man was in front of him, pulling out a throw-away lighter, and ripping his jockeys further down, lighting a flame and turning it up until the gas seared like a blowtorch. And in his agony, and misery, and the stinking mess, he did as he was told, knowing that he was never going to see Francine, or Stevie, or his mother ever again. He was dead meat. Dead meat that had also died of shame.

The airfield owned by Grigore Aman Ballistic Systems was eight kilometres outside Visina, in a flat and desolate part of southern Romania. Here the arms dealer's hangars were the highest parts of the landscape – two humps among the rapeseed. Further to the south were the Suceava mountains that divided Romania from Travonia; in between, the airfield control tower monitored both the air space and every field, dyke, road and track for kilometres around. No one could approach the GABS complex without being seen by radar or by surveillance camera.

That morning, while ground crew were active in Hangar One, a single-decker bus drove along the road from Visina town, watched all the way by control-tower staff. It stopped eight hundred metres away at the gates of the airfield. Seen sharp and clear on the TV screens, the bus was searched: outside, inside and underneath. The seven men sitting in it wore green overalls, looking as if they were coming in for a day's work, although some seemed on the old side for that.

The bus was cleared, entry permission was given, and it drove through the heavy gates. Within minutes it pulled up outside Hangar Two where its passengers, carrying suitcases and hold-alls, got off and were taken into the building. At the rear of the hangar stood an old prop Anson, a typical flying motor coach. At the front, neatly spaced between screens, were seven camp beds, each with its own side locker and light.

Grigore Aman himself came into the hangar and greeted the men in the common Roma/Travonia language of the region. 'I hope you'll be comfortable while you're here.'

Some looked as if they doubted that – but others waved aside trifling talk of creature comforts. They started unpacking – clothes, bedside alarms, books, newspapers, small ornate crosses and Orthodox images of a suffering Christ.

'I welcome you today as exiles from your own land. I shall salute you on Friday as members of the Southern Travonia Neo-Vlach government.' Grigore Aman was slight and smooth, and could have been a travelling salesman in silk underwear. 'I was right, was I not? Visina town has been a safe Romanian haven for a while…'

'It has – but the south of Travonia will soon be safe also,' said one of the men in green overalls, slightly younger than the rest.

'Good luck to that,' Aman said as he turned away.

'I think we pray,' a frail soon-to-be government minister announced. 'To our Lord and Saviour for our safekeeping, for the souls of those Christian soldiers we have lost, and to the success of our archbishop leader Zanko Boev in the final act of deliverance.'

They bent their heads and the hangar echoed with loud amens, before some zealots walked over to inspect the Anson that would fly them to Zoltzhim in southern Travonia, Zanko Boev's chosen seat of government: which was to be renamed Dumitru, after Saint Demetrius.

Fifty metres away in Hangar One the MiG-23 Flogger was nearly ready. The centre-line fuel tank had been filled, the jets in the Zvezda ejection seat checked, the missile launchers primed, and their hardpoints strengthened and readied to receive a missile under each wing when the fighter arrived at the remote airstrip over the border in Travonia. All this was standard preparatory procedure. What was not, was the paint job being done on the plane. The markings that showed it to be a former Soviet Air Defence Force jet had been painted out, and in their place were the markings of the People's Liberation Army Air Force of China – red stars bordered in yellow. This would be Grigore Aman's 'out' if he was accused of providing a MiG Flogger for a hostile act in a neighbouring country. The plane would look like the start of a ceremonial Chinese fly-pass as it dived in for the final, devastating, Neo-Vlach terrorist attack at the next day's Celebration Concert.

13

'We kill him. We tie together the loose ends of his life, and we kill him.' Stoica sounded very certain about what had to be done. Zanko Boev's face was impassive. Tomescu was frowning, and Stefan Remes, with his laptop beside him, was shaking his head.

'We don't kill him yet, we need more help from him. Correct, we tie up loose ends. We tell his college he has gone to be with his sick father—'

'His *dead* father, in two days!'

'But at this moment we only take him off the scene. We text the father that there is a geography excursion to the highlands of Scotland – cellphones are often out of range in those mountains. But the mountains are eight hours away, he is not there yet, he may need to reply to his father in his special style.' Remes looked down at his laptop. 'His Facebook page is old – nothing posted for a month. But also we check with him.'

'That's me.' Stoica turned to go back to the bedroom.

'Wait. Later. When we hurt him next time we get every piece of information. We still need to know, does anyone come here – other students, football friends…?' Remes held up the West Ham ticket they'd found in the boy's wallet. 'Everyone. And what are his other commitments. Who is expecting him to meet them, anywhere? And when does his mother come back?'

'Why all this?' Stoica was standing with his feet apart, hands by his sides, still offering his special sort of service. 'Why not an accident, tonight. In the canal. On the road. Kill him like that and it takes care of everything. They all know then.'

'And who comes racing back from Travonia?' Remes asked. 'From Ireland? The father. The mother. Other family. All here. Don't be stupid, Otto.'

'Remes is right, for another reason.' Boev's voice was decisive. 'Hold off for a day, perhaps two. If things go against us we can barter with his life. Hostage. He could be an advantage to us. The money's very nearly pledged; some last calls and I go to sign over the order for the plane. We need only a short time…'

'And then we kill him,' Stoica insisted.

'Certainly then we kill him. There must be no witness to who was here, no evidence to implicate this head of state personally.' Zoev poked his own chest.

The others nodded their agreement. The boy would be kept alive, but not for any longer than it took to set in motion the final deadly attack.

* * *

In pain and degradation, lying there in blood and vomit, Charlie had messed himself now. He was shamed already at what he'd been made to do. He'd seen films of torture and interrogation, but no one could ever know how that poisons you inside. Charlie Peat was now the lowest of the low, the kid who had cracked instead of dying – and he despised himself for that.

Despised – but he was also filled with a wild anger that had him fighting against the flex, wriggling and squirming to be free, snorting to breathe through his blood-blocked nostrils, swallowing frantically behind the gaffer tape and nearly drowning in his own saliva. All he wanted was revenge. But he knew his puny strength would never get him released to take it. He had no chance, and he was mad to think he had. Worst of all was knowing that he'd got the answer to Ron Moreton that would have helped his mother to get better – and now she wasn't going to hear it for ages, by which time she'd have got worse, and worse…

The bedroom door was open; the boy's state could be seen along the passage from the sitting room, and he could be heard as he writhed in the mess he'd made. Boev sent Tomescu to check – who came straight out again, retching himself.

'He's stinking more than death. Kill him now – the stench couldn't be any worse.'

'Clean him up,' Boev ordered. 'Use the shower. Throw his clothes in the garbage and find others from his room.'

'Why me?'

'Because those are your soldier's orders,' Boev told him. 'Stoica is on watch downstairs. Remes is planning, with me. You can be spared for ten minutes. For his cause a soldier in a religious war has to do many unpleasant things.' There was a commanding expression on the Archbishop's face; the face of the next president of southern Travonia.

Without another word Tomescu took a deep breath and went to untie the ankle flex from the radiator, to drag the filthy boy to the shower.

He stared with fear up at this fat man who was pulling him into the bathroom. What was this? Was he going to be drowned, or water-boarded? All the way through one door and into another he twisted, straightened, kicked two-footed – but having his hands tied behind his back left him open, and when he arched his body to die fighting, another vicious punch in the groin jack-knifed him in pain.

The shower was big; this was no tight cubicle, more a

corner of a wet room. He was dragged in and the button pushed, sending down a stream of cold water. He was pushed under it as a switchblade cut off his shirt, jeans, and pants. The man made as if to cut off his penis, too, panicking him into the greatest writhing of his life, but the man's laughter brought one of the others, and after some rough foreign words the shower was turned off.

Blinking the water from his eyes, he saw the look on this other man's face, the thin-faced one who had hurt him before – giving a sort of lick of his lips as if this was the time for more torture, the second interrogation – because they hadn't cleaned him up to take him out for a walk, had they? This man with a face like an axe called one of the others, and the fat one was sent off with sponges and towels.

'We need more information.' It was the man who spoke good English, although Charlie was not allowed to see his face. They rolled him off the drain while his blood and filth was sprayed away; and, shivering there on the floor-tiles, terrified of what the vicious man was going to do, he cringed in the depths of shame and degradation as he told them what they wanted to know, so as not to get hurt any more.

Kill me, but please, please, no more pain...

* * *

Between bites at a banana, one of the secretaries at Victoria College took the telephone message. 'Did you say Charlie Peat?'

'Charlie Peat. P – E – A – T.'

'That's Twelve C, isn't it?'

'I think so.'

'And you're saying he won't be in?' She was calling up Charlie's details on the computer screen.

'I am informing you that he is flying to Travonia, his father is very ill…'

'And you are…?'

'I am in London.'

'No, what is your relationship with the student?'

'I am his uncle, speaking for his mother, who is not in London.'

'Yes, we know about her.' The secretary was frowning at the screen.

'He is flying to Travonia.'

'Could you give me your name, please?'

'Victor Peat.'

'Do his grandparents Mr and Mrs Julien know you are phoning?'

'Everyone knows. This is a very busy time, and I have been asked to telephone to you.'

'Which is very kind of you. Please give Charlie our

best wishes. But would you kindly ask his mother or Mr or Mrs Julien to confirm what you're saying in writing or by email?'

'Exactly what do you want them to say?'

'The fact that Charlie is going to Travonia to be with his sick father. This could then become an authorised absence and not count against his course attendance record...'

'Very good. Thank you.'

'You have our addresses – postal and email?'

'Of course.'

'Then we look forward to hearing from Charlie's guardians.'

But Stefan Remes had already hung up the landline phone in the Grove Road flat.

In the school canteen Bijan was shaking his head at the text he'd just received. It was from Charlie – who was sorry to be missing the testimonial on Wednesday because Stevie was ill, and he was getting ready to go to Travonia. He would catch up with Bijan when he got back to London. And that was it – except for the weird way Charlie had signed off. He always signed off with 'WHSF' – 'West Ham's Strongest Fan'. *Always*, never failed. While Bijan's sign-off was 'WCS' – 'Wing

Commander Shafei'. Again, *always,* never failed. They had used those initials for ever. Now, what was this? *Cheers, old man – Charlie?'*

'He's gone all Oxshot and Camshaft,' Bijan told Francine. 'Like a Cranwell cadet. I know his dad's ill, but...'

'The same for me. He's signed off like we're married. *All my love.'* Francine was blushing.

Bijan looked at his own message again, shaking his head. 'Funny, though – as in "not very".'

'Definitely.' Francine pulled a face at Bijan. 'As in, creepy,' just as the bell rang for their AS options, and the two went their separate ways, bagging their mobiles.

Sally showed Bridget the text she'd had from Charlie.

Bridget frowned. 'You could say it's short and to the point – like my old granddaddy's beard.'

Sally held the mobile to shield it from the May sunshine, read the message again. 'Stevie? Is this Stevie?'

'No, love, it's Charlie, bless him.'

' "Scotland"? He's going to Scotland?'

'And never a word about a field trip, till today. These academies, high and mighty, ruling the roost – never mind a bit of notice for the ma's and da's. My boy at home, I'd have to be shouting for the pants and socks off him…'

Above them, an aeroplane headed noisily for Stansted and nothing was said for a few moments. But Sally was saying nothing anyway. She had put her phone onto the bench beside her; she was rocking slightly, and frowning. 'Ron Moreton,' she said. 'Ronnie Moreton…'

'I know, sweetie, Charlie was on a mission for us, wasn't he? But he'll do it. He's a good boy. He won't forget. He'll bring himself back soon, and then he'll do it, I know he will, for certain.'

But Sally had closed her eyes and her head was bowed. 'Ron's off the scene,' she said softly into the shadow she cast on herself. 'My boy is just trying to please me…' And whatever Bridget might say after that, nothing could get Sally to lift her head again.

He was back in the bedroom – as trussed and helpless as before; except now they'd sat him with his back to the radiator. They'd tied his wrists to it instead of his ankles, and they'd forced him into a clean T-shirt and football shorts and left him facing the closed door with his mouth taped over again. But he was alive, and they hadn't hurt him after that last punch – although he knew they would at the end. Definitely. They were going to kill him, and that axe-faced terrorist would make sure it hurt like hell.

These men were terrorists, he'd worked that out. Burglars would have taken what they wanted and gone; kidnappers would have had him pleading for money down his mobile phone; a gang planning a heist would have just shut him in a cupboard. But these men were keeping him alive to help them with their own plans, getting on with some campaign; some terrorist campaign, it had to be. And not Al Qaeda – Muslim terrorists would look different, with beards, and the foreign words they spoke would have sounded more like the Muslim kids at school, who spoke fast. These people took their time speaking. And how they said 'Travonia' when they dictated his texts gave him a good idea where they came from. *'I'm off to Travonia to be with my dad.'* They said it with their own rhythm, quick, certain – the way people said it out there. And what they knew about his dad being in Travonia made it all the more likely. These men had to be terrorists from Travonia. The bloody cowards! Like Al Qaeda, these bastards were fighting dirty. They didn't stand up soldier to soldier, army against army, they skulked in the shadows and set off remote bombs that were meant to kill anyone unlucky enough to be in the wrong place at the wrong time. How brave was that! How bloody brave!

The boy's BlackBerry made a sound. It was lying on the table in the sitting room, close to Remes at his laptop. He opened it to read the text.

```
Charlie — long time, no hear. Are
you OK?
Saw the Hammers report online.
Were you there?
Poor old Irons. Keep in touch, Kid.
Home soon, though — flying out on
Sunday 8th May, after the big gig
on 6th.
Love to Mum and the Groans.
Dad.
```

After a word with Zanko Boev, who was still raising funds down in the studio, Remes went to the boy and made him send a reply to Stevie, dictating the meaning and watching him work on it.

```
Sorry — got to be quick. Off to
Scotland on a geography field course.
```

```
Sir says there's no cellphone signal
where we are.
Will text you when I'm back.
Charlie, your loving son.
```

Stevie frowned at what he was reading. 'That's not right,' he muttered.

'Words not coming?' Deano asked. 'Can't fit them in? Well, don't start thinking I'm changing my tune – I'm dead set on that top line.'

They were in the back of a taxi, coming back from a first look at the Dynamo Naraiova Stadium. The splitter van was parked at the venue, so three taxis had been provided at government expense.

'Melody schmelody!' Stevie told him. 'Got a text from Charlie – and he's gone all Eton College on me. How would you react to getting a message from "your loving son"?'

'Stitched up – 'cos I haven't got one, so far as I've been told. What, is he asking for money?'

'Nope. Going to Scotland on a field trip. And he says "Sir says there's no cellphone signal."'

'Which caught me in the Trossachs once. Painful! The man must know.'

'Well, that's it again. Charlie's geography teacher's a

"Ms", not a "Sir". She's Ms Pearson – a delightful sight on open evenings, too…'

'Maternity leave,' Deano said. 'Up the duff from one of the lads and Sir's standing in…'

'Then, why "cellphone"? We never go on about cellphones, we say mobiles…'

'But they do out here. And Charlie was out here, wasn't he? He's texted the words he thinks his dim old dad's going to understand.'

'You cheeky little tyke.'

'I've had a text, too.' Paul Stoner was up front with the driver. 'My dear old duck – my mum – she's texted me to take care out here, because her *Daily Mail*'s on about a terrorist attack in Travonia.'

'That was weeks ago…'

'She's telling me to check under our stages and behind all the loudspeakers.'

'Security very good,' the taxi driver turned to say. He was a youngish man in a flat black cap, wearing a large photograph ID round his neck. 'Army all over, concrete blocks, steel fences. Not even tank get through. And special cars only inside cordon.' He lifted his ID, proudly.

Stevie and Vikki had gone over all this with the tour management. The splitter van wouldn't be allowed to drive in on the day; it had already been checked by sniffer dogs and forensics and was left securely at the stadium.

'Anyhow,' Deano twisted to Stevie. 'The song. We gonna run through the second verse tonight?'

'Sure,' Stevie said. 'If I ever get it written.' He looked away as if he were talking to someone else. 'But this one's got to be so dead right…'

14

Nearly all the money was in the bag, the basic sum for the MiG to be delivered which had to be paid over to Grigore Aman Ballistic Systems. The money was sitting in the Bucuresti Bank in the City of London, and the next morning Zanko Boev would go to there to sign the money order authorising the bank transfer. Now Tomescu and Boev were making last-ditch attempts to raise the balance needed for the most efficient means of attack on the Dynamo Stadium. This was all about the missiles to be deployed on the MiG Flogger. Aman wouldn't supply computer-directed Firecrackers without an extra final sum being paid over, so these armaments were being sent by road to a remote airstrip over the border, with the lorry of 'turnips' ready to turn around and return to Visina if confirmation of full payment didn't come in time. The Neo-Vlach would then have to fall back on the manually fired Atolls that were already at the airstrip awaiting the fighter. But, one way or the other, what the Neo-Vlach money had bought from the arms dealer would blow away President Gheorghe Ardeleanu of Travonia and the Chinese trade delegation the following afternoon, together with thousands of loyal supporters of the Power. After confirmation of the attack, Boev, Tomescu and Stoica, with their French passports in their pockets, would drive from the Grove Road flat to Stansted, and fly to Travonia's second airport, in the south of the country. The final reckoning was in sight.

Tomescu was puffed up, but sounding critical. 'After all we've done, we've got to be sure to hit our main target.'

'Thank you for that, General,' Stoica sneered, but Boev reassured the man who had raised most of the money.

'Our pilot is skilled. Even without computer guidance he'll hit his target, he's trained for it. The Chinese circus troupe goes onto the stage at 16.30. This is the climax of the celebration; this is when everyone is in place. If special guests have been taking refreshments they'll be in their seats for the Chinese performers, just before the official speeches. Our man will sight his missiles – and we shall change the future of Travonia.'

'Where's the stage set up?' Tomescu asked, looking at the aerial photograph on the living-room floor.

'Here. At the east side of the stadium, so the sun is in the performers' eyes, not the audience. Ardeleanu and his guests are facing the stage on a platform in the middle of the pitch here.' Boev's hand was shaky. 'The stadium is Dynamo Naraoiva, not Real Madrid. It's for athletics also, so it's wide and shallow with perhaps fifty tiers of seats.' His eyes left the photograph to look at the others. 'And this is very good for us.'

'Don't you worry, Tomescu,' Remes cut in, 'because it's not your worry. Our attack's going to surprise and devastate, and its result will shock the world. That's what we want, isn't it?'

'See, the seating isn't too high,' Stoica spelt it out like a teacher for a stupid child. 'The sides are like a soup bowl – you know, "soup bowl"?' He made the shape with his hands. 'Not a tall pot, so even without computer guidance, the Flogger can fly in over the city outskirts at roof level, get in undetected without needing height for a steep descent, and in it comes low, dive-bombing out of the sun – and the Power will never know what hit them.'

Tomescu grinned. 'They won't be expecting that.'

'Not after the false messages we've allowed them to pick up,' Remes said. 'They're searching vehicles like accident investigators.'

'I should get back to the phones,' Tomescu volunteered. 'Firecracker missiles can be locked on from miles away...'

Boev rubbed his hands together, the elderly veins like blue cords. 'So it is "go". Tomorrow morning the full amount for the MiG-Flogger will have been paid to Aman, our pilot believes the Viking rescue boat is ready, and he's at the airstrip now, waiting...'

There was a moment's silence.

Stoica bent his fingers and cracked his knuckles. 'So if everything's ready – when do I kill the boy?'

'Let me think about that,' Boev told him. 'After we have prayed. First, we pray.'

And the ultra-devout Neo-Vlachs kneeled, there in the living room in view of the boy, and raised their eyes to the demountable cross of Christ.

Francine was bright. She had taken twelve GCSEs and her results sheet had shown mostly A stars. She was persistent, too, her wrists often aching over her keyboard to get a chord sequence right. And brains and persistence paid off when she asked for Charlie's latest address from one of the school secretaries. This was Mr Danes, who kept even the principal in line. She caught him in the reception area heading for the office.

'You know I can't give you that, young lady. Not without the parents' permission.'

'He's not with his parents. He's living with his grandparents, while his dad's on tour. I know it's in Leytonstone somewhere.'

'Which alters nothing.'

'Then would you phone and ask them if I can have it? Please?'

Mr Danes walked on towards the office door. 'Sorry, no. I should get no work done at all if I spent my day making phone calls for students.' He reached for the door handle.

'OK. I'll ask Mrs Pritchard. She'll want us to support Charlie with his father so ill...'

Mention of the principal slowed Mr Danes. 'I wasn't aware...'

'Charlie's flying out to Travonia to be with his father. It must be bad.' She held up her mobile phone. 'And he's not well himself – he doesn't sound it – and before he goes I want to see him, to tell him how much we all care.'

Mr Danes pursed his lips. 'Wait there.' He went into the office and came back with a Leytonstone address written on a Post-it note. 'Please give him our best wishes.'

'Thank you.'

'Remember, I didn't give you that.'

'I'll tell them I used the Freedom of Information act.' And Francine headed back to the sixth-form common room.

The door was answered by a woman who had to be Charlie's gran, the female Groan. She looked at Francine and Bijan as if they might be trying to sell gas and electricity.

'We're friends of Charlie,' Francine got in quickly. 'We've come to see him before he goes.'

'Charles? Goes? Goes where? He's gone, girl.'

'To Travonia? Already?'

'No! His father came back from Travonia.' Charlie's gran shrugged. 'Charles doesn't live here any more.' She stared behind Francine at Bijan. 'Is this some joke, or student prank?'

Bijan edged himself in beside Francine. 'Mrs Julien, we're hearing Stevie Peat is ill in Travonia, and Charlie's flying out there to be with him…'

The Groan frowned. 'You're well out of date, boy. Charles's father is back home, in their own place. Grove Road, Mile End. I tell you, the man has come home now. And Charles is with him. His granddaddy took the last of his truck right over there a few days back and had a talk with him.'

Bijan turned to Francine. 'And Charlie came to West Ham from Mile End last Saturday…'

'Thank you, Mrs Julien.' Francine smiled at her. 'We've got it all wrong. We're very sorry to have bothered you…'

'Oh, it's no bother. Our ministry here on earth is to care for one another, praise the Lord.'

'And mine's to get on the tail of friends who shut us out of their lives,' Bijan said, as he walked away.

But Francine didn't go along with that. 'There's something up,' she said, 'apart from his mum. Something. This doesn't sound like the Charlie-boy I know…'

The boy's BlackBerry rang and rang – but Remes wouldn't answer it; the caller was 'Francine', and people usually text when they can't speak to someone. He didn't have to wait long; a bleep soon told him there was a message on the smartphone.

```
Charlie — I'm coming over to see you
tomorrow morning. I've got a free,
and I want to know what's happening.
Are you OK? Because it doesn't sound
like it. I know you're back at your
own home. The phone line's engaged.
```

The operator says there's talking on
it, so I know someone's there.
If you don't answer the door I'm
knocking up the neighbours to get
some info. So be there, Charlie-boy!
Love,
Francine x

Remes swore, and called Boev up from the studio. Along
the passage the boy could be seen bound and gagged, his
back against the radiator. They had been keeping him
alive, there in the main bedroom where he could be seen
and heard. They had fed him a few spoonfuls of cold
baked beans; and pushed an empty Comfort bottle at
him for peeing. As well as keeping an eye on him, the
decision to keep the boy in there had been the sheer drop
outside, and the fact that the window was double glazed
and locked, with the keys in Stoica's pocket – so even if
the boy somehow got himself free, the only way out of
the room was through the door.

Stoica was also called up from below, and the three
men stood looking at their captive as they discussed the
text message.

'Just text back to her, tell her he's at the airport, there's
no point in coming here.'

'And if the landline is checked again?' Remes asked. 'The operator will report talking. We have to use it if we want the last of the money for Firecrackers.'

'I don't like the landline being checked,' Boev growled. 'Do something to quieten this girl. Tomorrow morning I go to the Bucuresti Bank. After that, everything is "go", Firecrackers or Atolls. Then we leave this place, go to the airport, and to our rightful destiny. We need a few hours, that's all.'

'So she comes, and we send her away content,' Remes suggested. 'End of the story.'

'End of the story,' smirked Stoica.

From the bedroom Charlie saw Axe-face come up the stairs and stare at him with two of the others. Every time one of them came near him his skin froze over, his stomach ran to water again – but with this one it was worst of all. He was violent, he wouldn't hesitate to kill him. And killing him would kill his mother, too. Whatever Ron Moreton's problems had done to her, she'd be a million times worse when she found out her Prince was dead. And as the man came along the corridor there was a look in the bastard's eyes that said he'd come for a killing. This was the end – and hell, it was going to be now! *It was going to be right now!*

He had no insides any more, his heart thumped hard, his eyes stared themselves dry as he watched them come along the passage towards him – and he started the fight of his life to get free. He twisted, squirmed, arched and kicked. He tried to scream and yell, but he could only moan behind his gag, and gulp and swallow. *He was going to die!* These men were coming along the passage right now to kill him. *God, help me!* He wriggled, stretched, thrashed out two-legged. And he cringed – cringed from what was coming.

But the men stopped inside the bedroom doorway. One of them, the man who spoke the best English, came one step nearer.

Charlie whimpered. The man had folded his arms like an executioner.

'You will listen. To me. You will listen to me very hard and you will do what I tell you.'

Charlie listened. God, he listened.

'Tomorrow you will choose clothes, and you will dress normal. You will stand inside the door when the girl comes.' He held up Charlie's BlackBerry. 'Francine. When she comes, she does not come inside. You will stand back. You will tell to her, go away, to leave you alone. You have private troubles. You understand? *Private* troubles. And you shut the door. Tell her she has to go away, if she has any care for you.' He bent forward. 'We will have this man behind her, on the street.' He twisted and pointed. 'This man' was Axe-face. 'If she does not go, she comes inside. And…' He cut his own throat with the side of his hand. 'You understand, uh? What we will do to her?'

Behind him Axe-face leered. It wouldn't only be the final killing of Francine that he'd enjoy.

Charlie swallowed. He nodded. He understood.

'OK. So you know what you are going to do? Or what we will do?'

Charlie nodded his head off.

'OK.'

There were noises from the stairs and the fat man came puffing through the doorway. He spoke mostly in their own language. 'Confirmation. The Firecrackers are on the road, if we have the rest of the money in place. But the MiG-Flogger is ready to fly from Visina tomorrow after the bank order is signed – will be inside Travonia in good time. And the back-up Atolls are in place.'

At which he was shushed, but they were all nodding as they turned away – except Axe-face, who stared hard at Charlie, and slowly showed him his tongue.

The No Rider sound check went well, everything

considered; the Dynamo Naraiova Stadium was alive with troops and police, looking under seats, checking out changing rooms and pointing sniffer dogs at every piece of electronic equipment. There were no stage lights on, and an atmosphere was hard to whip up, but that was always the case with sound checks. Winny took each of their instruments in turn, listening to a few chords and adjusting the gain and equalisation. After they'd all set their own IEM monitor levels he got them playing 'Fervour' – which went out into the stadium with all the pop of flat cola.

'That was all shite!' he told them, 'but I'll get it sorted. All the levels are rodge.'

Stevie came to the front of the stage – which was being hung with velvet drapes. 'Winny, I'm going to run my solo…'

'Ta-ra!' Deano flourished, ready at keyboards.

'We'll clear off and hit the rider, then,' O'Hara said. 'Let the maestros have their moment.'

But he stayed at the side of the stage with the others as Nicky waited for a sign from Winny and began a slow rhythm with a soft brush on a snare drum. In came Deano's keyboard, muted and easy, and then Stevie approached his microphone, looking into it as if he was doing an interview.

'What do you do in the fight to survive
When you can't get the grub that you need?
Who's gonna help to keep you alive
When the fat cats keep feeding on greed?
Eh?
What do you do when the sky's falling down
And you're freezing with nowhere to go?
Who's got a shed, or a bed in the town
When you're losing your heat in the snow?
Eh?
We need community, human-kind, friends we never
    know,
Else, it's gold dust when you're on the up
But street dirt when you're low.
Eh?'

Nicky suddenly hammered a side drum and doubled the beat. Stevie pushed his mouth nearer the mic and growled a verse out, fast.

'What do you do when death's near your door
And you can't pay the medical fees?
Who's gonna stump up to keep you alive
When humanity's getting the squeeze?
Eh? Eh?

We need community, human-kind, friends
*   we never know,*
Else, it's gold dust when you're on the up
But street dirt when you're low.
We need!'

He stepped back from the mic to a dead silence until O'Hara asked, 'Where's that come from? You're not singing that? You are after us getting paid, aren't you?'

'Cracking tune, though,' Deano said.

'Flashin' sticks.' Nicky threw one up and caught it.

Deano wrapped an arm round Stevie's shoulder. 'Top stuff, Stevie. Protest Peat! The VIPs won't know what the hell it's all about – but the raddies will. Feel better now?'

'Not a lot,' Stevie said. 'But everything's relative…'

15

Charlie was dead certain. He'd heard the fat one say 'Travonia' again, but it was what else he'd said that clinched it – the same as he'd heard the others say in the living room. In the jumble of their own foreign language he'd definitely heard the word 'MiG-Flogger', spoken in English, like an international brand. And Charlie knew what a MiG-Flogger was – a Russian missile-launching aircraft. Bijan was always on about historic fighters, poring over his *Aircraft* magazine – Messerchmitts, Spitfires, Lightnings, Phantoms, Jaguars, *and MiGs*; in another life a few days ago he'd laughed about a Flogger *whipping* across the sky. And *'Firecracker'*. They'd said 'Firecracker' twice, and a Firecracker was a missile, Bijan went on about all sorts of weapons, all the time. And the fat man had come up the stairs all pleased about something, and he'd said 'MiG-Flogger' and 'Firecracker' again. So Charlie was dead certain. With talk of 'Travonia' in the mix, these men definitely had to be Travonian terrorists, and probably the same bastards who'd injured his mother. And now he knew what they were planning next: some sort of missile attack from the air. But, where? In London? In New

York? Out in Travonia – where Stevie was?

And all the time he was tied up and chained to a radiator, and couldn't let on to anyone. He knew vital stuff! He could save people's lives! If only! If bloody only! The frustration sent him into another frenzy to get free, pulling, pushing, straining against the flexes until his heart raced and his temples bulged. But he was tied so tightly his feet were dead, and his hands behind his back felt as useless as old gloves. He was a prisoner who was never going to escape. After Francine had gone he was going to be killed. And God knew how much it was going to hurt, the ways Axe-face was going to make him suffer before he died. A fresh surge of fear sent him into a new spasm – but those flexes still held him tight, totally helpless. He couldn't move, he couldn't shout; there was nothing he could do to save himself, let alone save anyone else.

Unless... He stopped struggling to think. Was there just a chance he could say something Francine could grab hold of? He would only be allowed a sentence, but could he work some 'MiG' or 'missiles' code into what he said at the door? He tried to concentrate on that instead of on Axe-face – banging his head against the wall until he somehow knocked into himself a stupid, half-baked idea. *What if he pretended he was talking about guitar technique, something about Stevie Hendrix and his 'speciality'?* She'd know what that was, he was always on about it. Dive-bombing. And *Stevie* Hendrix, not *Jimmy* Hendrix, to get her puzzling even more. He could only try. But if these terrorists thought for a second he was trying to pass a secret message, they'd pull her into the flat – and she was dead, too. With worse to happen first.

God, he had to be clever.

He thought, and thought, and like every sleepless night when he couldn't solve some problem his mind went everywhere and back again, over and over and over. Different parts of his life came into his head, and then it was back to the beginning again.

There was his mother at Stage Left. When she'd thought he was going to find Ron Moreton she'd been on the up, just a bit. And he *had* found him. Not only that, he'd got the news that might have helped her to start getting better. Ron Moreton hadn't been killed, and his heart attack wasn't her fault – Ron didn't have to be on her conscience – but now she'd never know that; when she didn't hear from her Prince she'd really think the lights had gone out.

And there was his dad out in Travonia, miles away from home, making the money to help her get better.

When she was well again he could pick and choose his gigs to suit him, do more with Jools and Sol, that sort of thing. But, until that day, to keep her at Stage Left he'd have to tour in all the dumps thrown at him.

And Charlie Peat would never be on a Rubber Girders' album. They were the best new band around, and soon they'd be looking for someone else on rhythm guitar, because he'd have gone dead on them. Bloody literally.

Plus Francine would think he was a total idiot. She probably thought that already, and if she bothered coming here the way these men said, what was she going to think of him when he sent her packing?

Unless…

And he was back again, full circle. Thinking, thinking, thinking – and coming up with nothing better in the way of a coded message, not one that wouldn't put her in danger. Which was the last thing on this earth that he would ever want to do to that girl.

The Bucuresti Bank was nearer to Aldgate than Threadneedle Street. Boev's appointment was for 10 a.m., as soon as the bank opened for business. The appointment had to be kept promptly because today was Friday the sixth of May, and with three hours' difference between

Travonia and the UK, the Chinese Celebration Concert at the Dynamo Naraiova Stadium would start at one o'clock, London time. There might be some leeway on the timing, because the concert would run for nearly three hours, but all the same, the MiG-Flogger wouldn't be allowed to take off from Visina in Romania until after the money transfer had been made to Grigore Aman. MiGs can fly at Mach 3, but this flight would be low and subsonic to keep itself under Travonia's military radar, so it would take twenty minutes for the plane to arrive at the old Soviet airstrip the maps showed as farmland. Here at Zoltzhim in south Travonia a Neo-Vlach pilot would take over because Grigore Aman wouldn't compromise his business – or Romania – by sanctioning an attack piloted by someone on his payroll. Adding on a further twenty minutes for the Atolls to be mounted on the hardpoints – despite the last-minute pleading still going on, the Firecracker money didn't look like being achieved – and ten minutes' flying at low altitude from the airstrip to the target, the Neo-Vlachs still had time in hand, providing Boev didn't miss his bank appointment by being held up in traffic.

What the boy mustn't know was that Zanko Boev's bank appointment would leave them short-handed at Grove Road because Remes would drive Boev in the decorators' van, stopping in a back street to take off their painters' overalls.

Before they left they got the boy ready for the girl's visit, at whatever time she arrived. When they untied his ankles he couldn't stand – they had to support him – but with kicks and punches they manhandled him into the bathroom and held him under the shower. Standing tight around him they turned on the water, the hot running through quickly. The central heating was switched right down at the thermostat, but they'd kept the hot water on. They couldn't change the boy's clothes with his wrists tied behind his back – and he had to look fairly normal for the girl – so his hands were freed, his arms pinioned hard to his sides by tight grips.

They made him rough-dry himself, before they pulled him out of the bathroom and bundled him down the stairs to his own bedroom.

'What you wear?' Stoica asked, pushing the boy at a built-in cupboard. 'What right?'

The boy stood and stared at the cupboard, and got a slap around the head for not responding quickly. The Neo-Vlachs meant business, and no one was going to delay them in carrying it out.

* * *

Charlie did his best to be intelligent – with a chance like this, what could he wear to make it seem wrong to Francine; what would jump out at her as not being Charlie-boy? He opened the cupboard doors, desperate for an idea. Why couldn't there be a hated Arsenal shirt hanging up – or a Barry Manilow top? On the left-hand side hung his coat, tops, and trousers. On the right were his drawers of pants, socks, and shirts. They'd been turned over already, when these men had found his T-shirt and shorts. And there in the muddle he saw something a girl like Francine might frown at: a Victoria College sweatshirt from last year. No one wore these sweatshirts in Year Twelve; if his mother had been home it would have gone into a charity sack by now, because the sixth form was uniform free; and the last thing a Year Twelve or Thirteen would wear for meeting someone from Victoria was college uniform. Francine would stand at his front door and drop her mouth open.

Charlie picked it up, and pulled it on. The fat man had already found a pair of jeans over a hanger, which he threw at him. Then it was just a pair of trainers, pulled on without socks.

The men started looking at watches and talking amongst themselves. Did that mean Francine was coming soon? Or, the most terrifying thought – *how long had he got left to live?*

They hustled him out of his bedroom, changing grips, giving him over one to another, pushing him along the narrow space between the kitchen and the studio to take him back upstairs.

And, in a split second between the two of them changing grips, Charlie suddenly saw a wild half chance for a last hopeless attempt at saving his life – and sparing him the terror of execution by Axe-face.

The MiG-Flogger stood ready on the apron at the Grigore Aman base in Visina. Along from it stood the old Anson, still being fuelled for its flight to Zoltzhim, the new Dumitru, which would become the seat of the Neo-Vlach government sometime after 16.00 hours that day. The ministers-to-be were packed and ready to go. Some prayed, some walked around the apron, some were at their laptops, going over briefing notes for their new ministries. And one was on his mobile phone, promising a girl in Visina that he would soon be sending for her.

The delivery pilot sitting in the Flogger was a retired lieutenant colonel of the Russian Air Force, Anatoly Dotsenko, who was used to flying all marks of MiG.

He earned good money delivering fighters to the world's wars with no questions asked of him. Now he set his instruments to the destination using the global navigation reference he'd been given. It was a fine day, and visibility would be good for his final approach to the old Russian airfield over the mountains in Travonia. He had checked that the missile hardpoints had been adapted for either Firecrackers or Atolls – but they weren't his problem. What the end-user did with the plane was of no interest to him.

Diligently he did his cockpit checks, until he finally radioed the tower that he was ready to taxi for take-off. For this special local export the Visina skies were being kept clear, so there would be no waiting at the runway's end.

But now he was put on hold. Everything was ready here at Visina, but word had yet to come from the Bucuresti Bank in London. Dotsenko's boss Grigore Aman didn't believe in anyone's cause – like Dotsenko he believed only in money.

The fat one was sitting in his parents' bedroom with his back to the door, while Charlie was ready on the bed in his jeans and college sweatshirt. He had no doubt that Axe-face was outside somewhere, lurking ready to come up behind Francine when she rang at the front door. Half an hour before, the one who spoke the best English had gone over the drill.

'You get rid, uh? You open the door, but she does not come in. Does not! You tell her you have private problem, not for her. "Go please. Thank you." And you shut the door.'

And then Axe-face had breathed his foul breath into his face. 'If you not do this – I push her in. She die!' And he punched him in the chest, no warning, no pull-back, suddenly crashing him back against a wall, almost stopping his heart. 'You understand?'

Without breath or voice, he had nodded. Yes, he did understand! But he knew he'd somehow got to slip something of his own into the drill, he'd got to say something in code. Holding his ribs, he'd wheezed, 'She'll think something's up...if I do that...'

'Uh?'

'I've got to say something else...so she knows I'm not mental...'

'About what?' the good English speaker had wanted to know.

'About my music. She's my music friend...'

Suspicious looks – at one another, and then at him.

'Three, four words. Three, four music words only.'

'And no "Help!" or she is dead.'

'Or she is dead!' And there had been that filthy tongue poked out again.

And they'd left him with the fat man, who told him to 'Shuddup!' and sit on the bed – pulling the dressing-table stool across the bedroom door and sitting on it.

The Bucuresti Bank wasn't busy. Zanko Boev was expected, and his meeting with the bank manager began promptly a few minutes after ten o'clock, London time. With Remes at his side Boev gave the number of the bank account into which Travonian immigrant workers had made their donations. It was a smallish, scruffy office, and smoking a yellow cigarette and flicking the ash into a paper cup, the bank manager himself called up the account on his desktop computer.

The conversation was all in numbers. Boev's account number, the collection account number, and the Grigore Aman Ballistic Systems account number in Visina. It was then tap, tap, tap, a draw on the cigarette, flick ash – the bank manager was boss in his own bank – and, 'OK.' He swivelled his monitor to show Boev the transfer of funds, completed. He signed a letter of confirmation – and within fifteen minutes the two Neo-Vlachs were heading towards Mile End, stopping just once to change back into their painters' overalls.

Grigore Aman came out of the brick-and-concrete office block and walked over to the MiG-Flogger sitting on the apron, the turbojet engines warmed to operating temperatures. And with two thumbs up to the cockpit, he gave the word. Waiting only a moment for clearance from the apron crew, Lieutenant Colonel Dotsenko opened up both engines and took the fighter out to the end of the runway. The sky above was clear of air traffic and radar told the same story, right up to thirty-five thousand feet. With no queueing for take-off, the fighter swung round to face down the two-kilometre runway – and within seconds permission was given for take-off. Dotsenko released the brakes and thrust the plane along the concrete airstrip, quickly reaching the 270 kph lift-off speed and immediately taking it into a steep climb at 330 metres a second. But he soon levelled off because he had to keep close to the ground and head for a careful crossing of the Suceava mountains, which would be like climbing up and over them. The sun shone down from the cloudless sky, but the MiG-Flogger cast no shadow, it was flying too fast for that.

The deal was done, the mission was a 'go', and the fighter was about to be delivered to the Neo-Vlach pilot who that day would kill the president of Travonia, and countless others in the Dynamo Naraiova Stadium.

16

The stadium was filling, but not nearly as fast as it would for a Sunday football match. Security checks today were rigorous with queues at every entrance, and the artists' and VIP cars going into the underground car park could only crawl through. Entry through the chicanes of concrete blocks was restricted to vehicles showing the special 'on-the-day' windscreen ID; even then, at the final checkpoint, and staring into an MP5 automatic, each passenger had to produce a concert pass and a passport.

Stevie had his two guitars in the cab – he never left them at venues overnight, and neither did O'Hara and Stoner. Nicky Harris had his drumstick case and Deano always kept the Jump Drive to his keyboard in his pocket. The rest of the backline equipment was at the stadium, locked in the splitter van.

No Rider was dressed ready in black – from hotel to stage – with Deano's white frockcoat swinging on a hanger like a ghost. They'd be sharing a changing room with an opera singer and her retinue, the conductor and section leaders of the Naraiova Philharmonic Orchestra, the chorus colonel of the Travonia Army Choir, and the

Transylvania Pops heavy metal band, so Vikki had gone on ahead to get No Rider some reasonable space.

The cab made its way slowly through one check, then another, nearly scraping a concrete block as it took a tight corner on full lock.

'It's feels like ould Belfast,' O'Hara said. 'A gun at your head soon gets your fret fingers a'flutter. And hear that? He can bugger off before we go on.' It was the clack of a helicopter, circling low.

Nicky's fingers were drumming a nervous rhythm on his case of sticks. 'Look at these weapons – do they really reckon it's all goin' to kick off?'

'No problem.' The cab driver spoke for the first time since they'd left the hotel. 'Like I tell, not even tank get near. And army on buildings, even suburb, no rocket grenade from far way off. Dead safe, my friends. Dead safe.'

'An' you can choose which one of those words you want to put your wages on,' said Deano.

The MiG made a bumpy landing along the airstrip. The concrete runway had been laid in the Cold War, but kept there afterwards as a handy road between the fields of rapeseed. Six weeks before, a Neo-Vlach cell had put tubs of rhododendrons along its length to camouflage it from the air – and had taken them away that morning.

Dotsenko came in low and slow at 90 kph, using the drag chute to stop the plane before the concrete ran out. He taxied the plane to the camouflaged awning that was stretched between trees at the airstrip's southern end, where two Atolls sat in their racks waiting to be loaded. There was no navigational setting to do on these missiles; they would be aimed and fired by the pilot. The Travonia Air Force major waiting to take over wasn't on a mission to hit a ship's hull – 'fire and forget' – but to target a VIP podium with a blast-frag high-explosive warhead. And his accuracy record was excellent.

This Major Ken Rahovei was younger than Dotsenko, but he knew MiGs very well; only that month he'd been flying a more modern mark in NATO combat conditions. He checked through the cockpit before he gave word for the transfer of the first missile to its hardpoint under the starboard wing; when he was satisfied, he signed the plane's log book, and patted the other pilot on the back.

'Thanks. You're doing our country a great service.'

Dotsenko looked at him as if he was a conscripted recruit. 'Who cares about your country?' He patted his battledress pocket. 'I fly for euros.'

'And I fly for a Neo-Vlach state.'

Dotsenko walked off, to the truck that had brought the Atolls through the Suceava mountains.

'You'll see!' Major Rahovei muttered after him. 'This is the start of the new Eastern Europe.'

He wanted to pee. God! Why did he want to pee now, when it would cost him a punch and a kick? And they'd have to let him do it, or Francine would see his wet jeans when she came to the door. *When she came to the door.* His stomach rolled, because when she did, he had to take his one chance before the end of everything. It was scary, a million times more than scary. Sitting on the bed, he was half up at every sudden sound, at every voice and at every car, and now he had to pee. He'd give it a hundred. He'd count a hundred, and then he'd ask for the bottle. He could just about hold on for a hundred...

But he nearly did it when the doorbell rang.

It hadn't stopped ringing before the fat man was on his feet. 'You do as told. You do all as told.' He gripped Charlie's throat. 'Not do – and girl is dead.' Pushing him, the man forced him along the corridor, into the living room, and over towards the front door. They were the only two there, him dressed in last year's school sweatshirt, and the fat man in his painter's overalls.

'Open. Back.' Said with a thump in the spine.

Charlie went towards the door, opened it wide, and stepped back.

Mile End. Fresh air. And Francine – but close behind her was Axe-face pretending to file rust off the railings with a wicked-looking rasp. His insides flipped. He wanted to cry. Francine looked great, stylish in an embroidered jacket and short skirt. Her hair was sleek, with a lick on her forehead. And she was smiling her special Francine smile at him. He felt weak; it seemed totally unreal that he was going to be killed in a few minutes, and his head swam as he saw the life he was leaving standing there looking so normal.

'Charlie-boy! Going to ask me in?' She was coming up a step, and behind her Axe-face was watching, ready to push her the rest of the way inside. Smiling.

'Sorry, France. It's all wet paint in here.'

She stared at his old sweatshirt, frowned, but nodded. 'We're worried about you, Charlie, Bijan and me. It doesn't add up. You said your dad's ill, you're going out to him – but he's playing the big stadium today. It's on the news, all that security against attack…high alert. And he got a mench on the news, with No Rider…'

Behind him the fat man coughed. Axe-face came up a step closer behind Francine.

'*Was* playing,' he said. 'He's ill.' They'd push her in

and kill her if she got suspicious. *Forget coded message, he just had to get rid of her, fast.* 'You'll have to go, France. Sorry. But *you* sing my song, with the band.' There – he'd said something after all – but he could hear both terrorists breathing hard.

Francine was half smiling, half frowning.

'You know – my new one, "Upside Down". Think about it, France.' It was a weak last chance. *Upside Down* instead of *Inside Out*. He shut the door on her – and stepped back into a dog's bite of a grip on his neck. His last sight of her was her shaking her head, that sad look of 'please yourself' she'd given him after he'd missed the first audition. But what she had just said was twisting his insides with a new fear: for his dad: *'All that security against attack…high alert…'* And it suddenly hit him. Even Travonian terrorists wouldn't be able to fly into British air space with a Firecracker; now he was dead certain where that MiG-Flogger with its missiles was heading.

On the speakers in the home-team changing room, Stevie and No Rider heard the Naraiova Philharmonic Orchestra playing Leonard Bernstein's overture to 'Candide', still a couple of hours away from getting onstage themselves. In the Directors' Bar they had eaten a light buffet, and on TV they had seen the arrival of the government party with their Chinese guests, parading to their places on the podium like world leaders who had just signed an international treaty. Now No Rider was in that fretting state between boredom and tension that always hits before a gig – when everything was ready and all they could do was wait.

It wasn't the calmest dressing room in the world. The Transylvania Pops were there with their leader lording it, the lot of them drinking already and taking up more seats than they needed. There were the baritones from the Travonia Army Choir, who'd decided this was a nicer dressing room than the gymnasium. And there were three bare-legged girls from the Chinese State Circus who had followed them in, miming that they'd lost their way, and staying. The real tension came from the armed police who stood stolidly at the door, letting people in but questioning any move to go out. Security was everywhere. Wrist bands were checked and re-checked, and Stevie had re-tuned his guitars twice after heavy-handed inspections to make sure his Stratocasters weren't loaded with ammunition. Every door, and every turn in every corridor, had its MP5 automatic.

'This is a bundle of fun,' Stoner said. 'Where's Dulwich Park when you want it? Good job I'm not the claustrophobic sort.'

O'Hara had closed his eyes. 'I'm walking the Belfast Hills,' he said. 'It's all in the mind...'

But Deano took Stevie to one side. He cocked his head at the speaker, specially installed for the artists. 'You sure about your solo?' he asked him.

'"Street Dirt"?'

'Yeah. They're going to get it all down here.'

Stevie looked up at the stage-to-dressing-room speaker and across at the security at the door, who were clearly from a crack squad like an anti-terrorist unit. Not much was going unnoticed – probably because it was the performers on the stage who'd be the best placed of all to strike at the VIPs.

Stevie leaned into Deano. 'I've got to do it, and it's only the start if I'm going to save my soul...'

Deano nodded; thought for a moment. '*Our* soul, Stevie. No Rider is all of us. But just mumble a bit, eh?'

All the pre-mission checks had been done on the MiG. Beneath each wing was a three-metre tail-finned Atoll, each warhead packed with cluster high explosives, each tube filled with enough propellant for the manual attack. The sight of the fighter, standing smart in its new Chinese livery, had got the ground crew stamping their feet with anticipation. Radio contact had been made with the Viking rescue boat that was set to pick up Major Rahovei after he'd evaded Travonia's fighter planes, ditched the MiG, and ejected into the Black Sea. He had set his navigation course to take him first to Naraiova and its stadium, approaching from the south and veering west some twenty seconds short, which would bring him out of the sun at the target. Everything was pinpointed; only the precise position of the podium needed a visual. Now everyone waited. A radar display and a television monitor were beside the MiG, shielded from the May sunshine, the TV telling them that the Chinese Celebration Concert had started. As soon as the band from Britain went onstage the MiG's engines would be fired up, eighteen minutes from the attack – when all the VIPs and President Gheorghe Ardeleanu and his ministers would be in place for the special Chinese circus finale.

And for the finale to the Power's anti-Christ control of Travonia.

Boev and Remes – house painters again – headed back in slow-moving traffic along Commercial Road towards Mile End. Both looked grim, but satisfied. The attack was on; now what lay ahead was a safe departure from Grove Road, the drive to Stansted, and the flight to South

Travonia, where Zanko Boev would soon be the leader of a new Christian Orthodox Neo-Vlach government. His face showed something of the responsibilities of what lay ahead.

Remes spoke in a reassuring voice. 'Everything is in place,' he said. 'Everything is taken care of...'

'Everything? The pilot?'

'Especially. He will ditch the plane, but as instructed there will be no pick-up launch. Cancelled. He will drown. He can never speak to tell anyone whose orders he was following. No one can prove he wasn't a rogue, a maverick, and the international community can't charge the president of South Travonia with crimes against humanity...'

'We had to do what we did,' Boev told him. 'For our cause, and for our brothers who are dead and in prison, already bearing the cross of the good Lord for us all.'

'And amen to that,' Remes said. 'Amen to that.'

17

The front door was shut. Francine had gone. Charlie daren't risk shouting out after her in case Axe-face grabbed her and pulled her inside. His only real chance had just gone. From the look on her face she thought he was stupid, so she wouldn't go running to the police. And these people had kept him alive only for the time it took to see her off – so now he was dead. He could only wait for them to do it. And when those missiles hit, his dad was dead, too. *Dear Jesus, he was scared!* He hated every bastard terrorist who'd ever lived. It was the lowest and dirtiest way any animal could ever fight.

Suddenly the doorbell rang again. *No! Axe-face had grabbed Francine and he was bringing her in. He was going to push her in through the door with his filthy tongue hanging out.*

The fat man had gone rigid behind him. He muttered something down in his throat.

The doorbell rang once more, longer, and a voice could be heard from outside – Axe-face saying, 'Sorry, wet paint. Not go in.' He called it louder, as if for the fat man to hear. 'Not go in.'

But a second voice was just as loud as his. Miss

Portland's. Maevy-baby's. 'We *are* going in. This is the caretaker. Jason, open the door with your key.'

Thank God! Miss Portland had come! Had what he'd done downstairs paid off? In his terror he'd forgotten the wild chance he'd taken.

'Stand away, mate,' Jason commanded. He went to the gym five times a week.

'One moment.' Now there was a loud knocking on the door. 'Moment. Moment. Lady is coming in. Lady is coming in.'

Charlie was twisted around and frog-marched fast along the corridor to the bedroom, the door was slammed shut, and the fat man pulled a knife on him.

'You shout – I come back, cut throat.'

He made the world-wide gesture, and out he went to thump his back against the door, standing guard.

Otto Stoica let the lady and the caretaker into the living room.

'So sorry. Wet paint.'

'Well, I don't care about wet paint,' the lady told him. 'Where's Mrs Peat?' She looked around. '*Sally?*' she called.

'People go out.'

'Well, we're having that boiler switched off before

there's an explosion, it's coming through the wall like a runaway train. Can't you hear the racket? What are you people thinking of?'

Stoica stared at the two unwanted visitors. His hand tightened around the rasp he was holding.

'I can't leave this door,' Tomescu called in Travonian from along the corridor.

'Lead on, Jason, you know where the boiler is; like mine.' Already the lady was pulling the caretaker down the stairs and towards the kitchen, suddenly stopping at the central heating thermostat opposite the boy's bedroom. 'Look at this! It's been turned up to tropical!' She went into the kitchen and opened the cupboard that housed the Baxi boiler. 'Turn everything off, Jason,' she instructed. 'Even if we're not all blown to smithereens, Mrs Peat's going to be hopping mad to find how they're quick-drying her new paint.'

The caretaker did as he was told; while the lady went to the whiteboard on the kitchen wall, took up the marker, and wrote, 'Sally – I've had these men switch off the central heating. It's <u>dangerous</u>. Talk later. Maeve P.'

'And don't rub that out!' she told Stoica. With a good look around the kitchen, and a wrinkling of her nose, she asked the caretaker, 'Is that secure now?'

'Yeah. I've over-ridden the system, they can do what they want to the thermostat. It's start-up sludge from the radiators.'

'Like always! I'll speak to Mr Peat when he's back. He's got to get it fixed.'

'Needs draining down and "resolving".'

'Whatever.' Now, and only now, did she leave the kitchen and lead the way back up the stairs. She passed Tomescu, who was standing with his back to the bedroom door that he couldn't lock; Stoica had the key.

'What colour are you going to paint this?' she asked him, sounding as if she was now prepared to be pleasant. 'What? Colour?'

But Tomescu didn't have a chance to open his mouth before the bedroom door suddenly swung open behind him. He nearly fell into the room as out of it came a woman looking like the photograph of the mother: shining black hair, blue eyeshadow, scarlet lipstick, long silk coat – and trainers.

'Maeve, baby,' she said in a cracked voice. 'Great to see you, darling.' And while Tomescu steadied himself, she hurried along the corridor, into the living room, and headed straight out through the front door.

'Sally!' The lady followed. 'I came about the boiler!'

'Off to Croydon!' the mother shouted over her shoulder – suddenly jumping down the steps like an athlete and running fast along Grove Road.

Stoica and Tomescu leapt down the steps after her, but they baulked on the busy pavement – where they stared this way and that through the shoppers and across the road thick with traffic, but there was nothing to be seen of the mother in her long coat. Straight off they were back inside, Stoica grabbing at essentials as Tomescu tried to raise Boev and Remes on their mobile phones.

'Musicians!' the bossy lady said. 'What a crazy way to run a household.'

After a short interval for setting up, the No Rider backline was in place and the guitars were given final tweaks. Winny Beckford was out front at the sound desk, and in their black shirts and one white frockcoat the band stood waiting in the wings of the arena stage, watching the act they'd follow. It was the opera singer Carmen Amorosi accompanied by an ensemble from the Nariaova Philharmonic Orchestra. Hers was a world-famous name, and the stadium audience was filling to capacity again after the break. She was singing 'One Fine Day' from *Madame Butterfly*, elegant and commanding in her long turquoise dress, her voice lifting the open stadium.

'Ten minutes,' Vikki told Stevie. She had the running order in her hand. 'Three songs after this, then we get on – thirty seconds for plug-ins, and then "Hold Back the Thames".'

Stevie turned to her. 'What time's the flight on Sunday? I'm ready for home.'

She looked surprised. 'Check-in, 14.00. But you give this gig some respect. I want an autumn tour.' She looked at him, hard, but he wasn't looking at her: all his attention was on his last-minute tuning.

Charlie pulled off the Roberta Flack wig and threw his mother's silk coat over a litter bin. He dodged between cars and ran across Grove Road into Mile End Park. Quick looks over his shoulder told him he wasn't being chased – but he put down his head and ran on towards the Regent's Canal, where he took a north turn along the towpath. He had to get to a police station, and fast. He hadn't got long, he knew that, he could be too late already – Travonia time was three hours ahead and any second his dad and hundreds of others could be blown up by a missile from a MiG. *He had to get out the alert!* If he'd had his BlackBerry he'd have called him direct;

but he hadn't, and it was no good trying to borrow one because he couldn't remember the number. He sprinted past the moored canal barges, through joggers and dog walkers, had to stop to pee behind a tree and swore at the time it took, then it was up the steps onto Roman Road – with no one in the freewheeling East End bothering to take any notice of a kid in jockey-shorts, lipstick and blue eyelids. But his body was cramping up fast; those hours of being tied at the ankles were starting to cripple him, and he was still swollen like a giant artichoke where he'd been punched in the groin. He ended up limping across side roads, through shoppers and around stalls until he made it at last to a right turn into Victoria Park Square.

His lungs were raw and his sweatshirt was steaming. He ran at the automatic doors of Old Ford Green police station, which opened slug slowly. But he was here! – although how long was it going to take to get the police acting on a terrorist warning from a half-naked black kid in women's make-up? MiGs could fly supersonic. Stevie could be killed at the concert without ever knowing how. Every nano-second was going to count – so he had to be quick getting his message across. But just look at him: what were the chances of that?

* * *

Stevie took his Stratocaster from the guitar stand and slung it over his shoulder. When Carmen Amorosi had taken her final bow she would walk off stage-left; No Rider would come on from stage-right. There were no front tabs, and being broad daylight there wouldn't be dry ice or a lighting 'reveal', so the band would be seen as they ran on, plugged in, and stood ready for the 'one-two-three-four'.

Stevie went to a peep-hole and looked out front. The sun was in his eyes, but he could see the VIP podium with its special guests all in place. In the centre of the dais was the Travonian president, Gheorghe Ardeleanu, a familiar face from magazine covers. He had Chinese visitors sitting on either side of him, and what had to be government ministers making up the rest of the front row. Beneath them amongst heavy security on the pitch was the standing audience, and all around were the seated tiers of the stadium bowl – everyone silent right now listening to Carmen Amorosi finishing her twenty-five minute set with the fiery 'Habenera' from Bizet's *Carmen*.

'L'amour, l'amour, l'amour, l'amour
L'amour est enfant de bohème…'

Stevie turned to look at the stage, and he swallowed.

' "Love"…' he told O'Hara. 'Sal used to sing that to me when we first dated. You should've seen those flashing eyes…'

'And you'll see 'em again, bucko. You'll see 'em again.'

'That'd be good,' Stevie said. 'God, wouldn't that be good?'

Charlie squeezed through the automatic doors.

'Terrorists! Missile attack!'

He tried to sound urgent and believable both at once – but straight off he was rugby-tackled by a young policeman.

'Not me! Not here! In Travonia!'

He was pinned to the floor. All he could see were black boots, all he could hear was shouting and screaming and doors slamming.

'Stand away!'

His T-shirt was pulled up his back, and his jockeys pulled down.

'Is he belted up?'

'Get off! It's not me!'

'Clean. Get up, fellah.'

He was pulled to his feet, his chest still heaving from his run.

'It's not me…I've escaped…I've been a prisoner…I

was going to get killed. They're bombing a concert in Travonia! Air attack!' He'd got to convince them he was telling the truth – and fast – because that concert was happening today, now, with his dad there!

'Eye gloss and lipstick?' The policeman who had thrown him to the floor was staring into his face. 'You students got a Rag Day or something? Because if you have, sunshine, it's not funny.'

'It's true!' Charlie shouted. 'Four men held me prisoner. In Grove Road.' He tried to point in the direction of the flat, but his arms were pinned tight. 'From Travonia. Terrorists! And…they're…doing…a missile attack…' He shouted at the police as if he was convincing idiots. 'Firecrackers!'

'Yeah. Someone's crackers for sure. They've sent an AC/DC student to come poncing in here to tell us all about it…'

'They're bombers. Dressed up as painters.'

'Hang on.' An older policeman wearing sergeants' epaulettes on his shirt moved the first man aside. 'You're going to have to make a statement. Then we can decide what to do about it.'

'*There's not time!* My dad's out there. Travonia! Stevie Peat and No Rider. They're going to bomb a big arena concert with a MiG-Flogger!'

'Yes, son, we'll have all that in your statement.'

'But there's not bloody time!'

'There'll have to be, won't there?'

Charlie was shaking with fear and frustration and anger. He threw his head back and shouted at the ceiling, trying to hit out in all directions with his fists and his feet. 'It's a 9/11 emergency!'

'Yeah, you said.'

They pinioned him tighter and took him struggling and shouting into an interview room.

'Lady-boy!' said the young policeman, and blew him a kiss.

Four hundred kilometres south of Naraiova, Major Rahovei was ready for take-off: ejection seat at amber, throttle-friction tight, trim set, fuel pump on, tanks full, mixture rich, flaps set, instruments zeroed, harness tight, canopy locked closed, altimeters set, controls unrestricted, weapon sights lit – and firing safety catches on, with the Atolls primed. His face was calm, he had a fighter pilot's nerve – a man about to fly solo to change the future of a country. He turned to the ground crew beneath the awning and gave the final thumbs-up. The attack on the Dynamo Naraiova Stadium was a 'go'.

* * *

Charlie wouldn't sit. He told the sergeant over and over how thousands were in danger, and he kept on saying 'Travonia' to try to drum it in. Hadn't they seen the papers, been on the internet? The concert and the threat was in the news. Didn't they know about the Travonian terrorists, for God's sake, had they forgotten the London bombs? His own mother had been hurt.

'So…' The sergeant sat, and pulled a statement form from a drawer.

'Name?'

'Charlie Peat…' Just the sight of the form told him this was going to take for ever – by which time the attack would be over and his dad would be dead. *What the hell could he do?* How could he get through to this stupid, pen-pushing man? And then he saw the blood on the back of his right hand, fresh, running down from where the police manhandling had torn the raw skin. He looked at his other wrist and down at his ankles: and there they were – big inflamed weals, bluey-red from being tied up with flex – and obvious enough for even this stupid sergeant to see.

'Look at these! Look! Do you think I'd do this for a Student Rag?'

The sergeant stood and stared at him. 'You're not into bondage, son? Or self-harming?'

'*No, I'm not!*' He waved his wrists again and lifted his ankles. How to convince him? He knew! He pulled his jockeys down. 'And am I going to punch myself this hard in the goolies?'

The sergeant winced at what he saw.

'I've been tied up for days. I've been punched and kicked!'

'Straight up?' the sergeant asked. 'Straight up?'

'Straight up!' He pointed a long, shaking arm at the sergeant. 'And what about you? Do you want to be a traffic cop or a bit of a hero?'

18

Carmen Amorosi had her bouquets in her arms, and was waving and blowing kisses as she dropped a last, deep curtsey. On cue behind her, No Rider's backline crew ran onto the stage with individual guitar stands and Deano's keyboard; on a thumbs-up from Vikki, the announcement boomed out, in English for the TV.

'Please now be welcome to Travonia popular British band – come back each year to our country of enterprise, special guests of the Power – applause please to…No Rider!'

Stevie groaned, stared down at the stage boards, shook his head.

'Go!' Vikki called.

Nicky Harris was ready first, his drum kit already out there on its riser. O'Hara pushed Stevie in the back and the rest ran on. They plugged in, checked their IEMs, and stood ready waiting for the word from Stevie. To polite applause he counted them in – and off went No Rider with 'Hold Back the Thames', their take on the *Daily Mail*.

'Shut the river
Raise the boom
Send them back
We ain't got the room...'

It was sung fast and with a heavy beat – in the middle of which O'Hara shouted across at Stevie.

'They're dead! You can't do "Street Dirt". They'll pick up every word.'

But Stevie didn't seem to hear; his head was tilted high, he was more snorting than breathing, and his face had the look of a man not so much playing his Stratocaster as seeing off his demons, doing pull-offs on the frets, more Jimi Hendrix than Jimi Hendrix.

Deano flashed a look across at O'Hara and shouted, 'Who put something in his milk?'

'Come upstairs,' the sergeant had thrown down his pen. 'Talk to my Chief Inspector. And I'll get you some first aid.' Supporting Charlie, he took him up the stairs – followed from the first landing by a woman in plain clothes.

'I was coming down,' she said. 'Is this the young man talking Travonia?'

'Yes, Ma'am.'

The sergeant knocked on a brass-plated door; the three were called in.

'He's got to listen!' he told the woman.

'He will.'

The Chief Inspector was uniformed, and black. He seemed to be expecting this. His eyes were sharp, giving him a once-over, head-to-toe, then toe-to-head.

'This young man has injuries commensurate with being tied and beaten,' the sergeant said, 'and he claims it was terrorist perpetrators who held him prisoner in Grove Road.'

Charlie was already shouting at the new face. 'They're going to attack the Travonian stadium!'

'Calm, man. Deep breaths. You're saying Travonia?' The senior officer looked across at the woman.

'Yes! Travonia. There's a big concert. Today. In their capital.' He was trying to do as he was told, breathing deeply and somehow talking more slowly, but he had to get it all out. 'My dad's playing there with his band. Right now! These men kept me prisoner...' He showed the woman his injured wrists and ankles. 'They're going to attack the concert with a MiG and a missile. I heard them say so.' He sped up now, couldn't get it out fast enough. 'Today. Soon. They're three hours ahead. Flying a Flogger.'

The woman was tapping numbers into her iPhone. 'Travonia's an orange alert,' she told the inspector. 'Two London bombs and a manhunt in Tottenham…Hold this young man for now, he's a vital witness.' She hurried out of the room.

'*Hold me?* I've got to tell my dad! He's at the concert! They're all a target!'

'What's his mobile number?' the Chief Inspector asked.

'Don't know – it's on my phone.' He shrugged at his lack of anything.

'What's the network?'

'O_2. BlackBerry.'

The man picked up the landline on his desk. 'Communications,' he commanded. He looked across at him. 'Be no good if he's on stage, though, will it?'

'Nothing's any good if you're not bloody quick.'

'What's his name?'

'Stevie Peat.'

'"Stevie Peat",' the officer said into his phone. 'O_2 network. I want the mobile-phone number, top priority.' He went to the door and called along the corridor. 'Could someone kindly get my visitor a Coke?'

Charlie started to feel dizzy and sat down, his legs twitching with delayed shock.

'My colleague's onto the top people. She's...' the officer made a circle in the air, as if taking in the whole of the Metropolitan police. 'Things will start to move quickly.'

'I'll get a bandage for that wrist, sir. Can't do much about the other place.' The sergeant went out, as the woman came in again.

'We're getting on to it,' she said. Just for a moment Charlie's knees stopped twitching. 'Special Branch has alerted the Yard – the anti-terrorist squad – and briefed the Foreign Office, right to the top. Everything that can be done is being done.'

'And it's got to be!' His dizziness seemed to pass. Shouting helped.

The woman came over to him. 'We're not only about bag-snatching in Roman Road, you know. We deal with all sorts here.' She smiled. 'Well, just look at you for a start...'

'I had to dress up as my mum. To get out.' He stared at her. 'Thinking quick.'

'I just hope you got here in time.' Her iPhone bleeped; she turned and hurried out of the room wearing a worried frown, which wiped the boastful look off his face, fast.

* * *

The MiG-Flogger roared down the runway. Reaching take-off speed, Rahovei lifted the fighter in a steep climb to eight thousand feet and levelled off. The head-up display showed the coordinates of his target, the e.t.a. clear in blue numerals: eighteen minutes and twenty seconds to run. After a skilled manual attack, this timing would get him over the deep-sea ditching zone by 16.25 at the latest, no radar tracking him back to the airstrip, and sinking the MiG a kilometre-and-a-half down would keep its background free from investigation. Nothing had to get in the way of the establishment of the new Neo-Vlach state of South Travonia, which would be just the beginning of the new order...

Stevie's solo was in the last-but-one spot of the set, before the tempo picked up for the finish with 'Fervour'. The audience had been dead when they started but, as the band played on, more and more of them had got into the music, especially those standing at the front. The Chinese VIPs clapped along with the rhythms and the government officials smiled and nodded at each other at the wisdom of booking this British band.

'Spittle Pavement' came to its end and Sean O'Hara shouted at Stevie again. 'We're winning. Leave out "Street Dirt". Cut to "Fervour".'

But there was no sign that he had been heard. Stevie's eyes were closed, and his head was tilted even higher. The last chords of 'Spittle Pavement' beat around the stadium to generous applause. He stood still at the front of the stage as guitars were loosened in the other players' hands. Now for his solo, if he did it.

'Sing it, an' we're sunk,' O'Hara called.

But Nicky was in his own world at the back, and 'Street Dirt' started with the drum, the slowly brushed three-four, and in came Deano on keyboard. O'Hara groaned. Stevie had opened his eyes, and was putting the mic to his mouth.

'My latest and last No Rider song,' he said over the intro. 'Cheers for everything.'

'Sweet Jesus, there goes next year!' O'Hara said – before he suddenly looked up at the sky.

Everyone else was looking up, too – intrigued, as an aeroplane came roaring in to make a pass of the stadium, a strike fighter, its wings and fuselage painted with the red star of the Chinese Air Force. It roared to the east and banked, and the Chinese VIPs stood with wide smiles to clap and to wave at it. The pro-Power stadium cheered, and Stevie put his song on hold.

'Take it from the top on my nod,' he shouted to Nicky.

But his voice was drowned out as from north, west,

and south, three Saabs suddenly roared across the sky on the tail of the Chinese fighter – all on collision course and closing at high speed. Cannons started to pump, people shouted, screamed, ducked, ran and pushed for the exits. This was no aerobatic display, this was war.

Security ran Stevie and the band off the stage as above them the four fighters looped and dived and went into G-force banks. Wing tip missed wing tip by millimetres. The Saabs harried, the strike fighter dodged, turbo-engines blasted and cannons went on pumping. The dog-fight dived, climbed, rolled – one second four jets hurtling towards the stadium, the next veering out across the tower blocks before banking and screaming back out of the sun again, the attack fighter seeming set to suicide crash, the Saabs looking too close to the ground ever to pull out. But fifty metres from disaster the lead Saab pilot rolled his plane and somehow tipped its wing under the attacker's starboard edge. With its trajectory skewed, the MiG had to abort its dive and pull into a vertical climb, the Saab sticking to its tail while the others fanned south and north, for whichever direction it tried for another attack.

But that attack never happened. As soon as the fighters were over the outskirts, the nearest Saab let loose with a heat-seeking Sidewinder, which screeched across

19

Charlie was put through to his dad's BlackBerry from the police station.

'Kid!'

'You're all right!' Charlie had never been so pleased to hear his voice. He was OK. The attack hadn't succeeded.

'We're loading our gear and getting out of here. How're you doing?'

'I'm good. But you won't believe this, I'm at Old Ford Green nick, and the main man here – the Chief Inspector – he wants to speak to you.'

'Charlie! What the hell've you been up to?'

'Not me, Dad – terrorists, the Travonian people who bombed Sol Newman's. They found out you were away, and they only bloody hid out in our flat. *Our flat!* And—'

'Shit, Kid!'

'But I'm all right, so's the flat, and I'll see you soon. I'm going to see Mum with some stuff I've found out: some good news about Ron Moreton...'

'What's that?'

'I'll tell you soon, but Ron's sort of OK and that's really good for her. Anyhow, here's the Chief Inspector to speak to you...'

'Sunday. I'm back the day after tomorrow. Not long.'

'Great. See you!'

Charlie handed the telephone over. There was a lot for his dad to be told, and it would be good if some of it was done by the police. And he ought to know who'd helped to stop the terrorist attack – but Charlie couldn't sing his own song about it, could he?

The stadium was still in chaos, but the No Rider crew was doing a professional load-out. Everyone was living for Sunday now. Only, down in the changing room O'Hara looked puzzled, and after Stevie had told him how Charlie had alerted the British police he was persistent.

'That's great from your boy, he's a hero, that one. George Medal, bucko, at least.' Now the frown. 'But what was that rubbish you were talking about your latest and last No Rider song? And flamin' "Cheers for everything"! You got me worried, out there.'

Stevie stopped casing his guitars and looked O'Hara in the eye. The room was bustle all around, but at this moment the two of them could have been in a soundproof booth. 'Listen, Sean. You've seen it, and I've seen it; it hits you every place we play. This country's the pits. Flashy cars run over beggars in the gutter and policemen step over them. People pay top whack for education and health care – or they have to make do with crap.' He took in a deep breath.

'Wealth is power, and I tell you – I'm deeply, deeply, ashamed of dancing to their capitalist tune. Palmer on Channel Four and Mary Queen of Scots at Posti were right; taking their money puts my snout deep in that very same pigs' trough.'

'Stop being so hard on yourself – and us. I've been over it with you, Deano's been over it with you. You did it for a reason, man, we all know that; an' we're all putting the money to good use. You will recall that my ould mum's an Irish Troubles widow…'

'Sure.' Stevie turned away to finish closing the locks on his guitar cases. 'I know that, Sean. But enough's enough. Listen, I've known for a few days now I don't want any more of it. I don't want to enjoy the perks the people who pay to see us can never get. You can't get away from it, exorbitant fees to keep Sally at Stage Left are no different from the profits these crook capitalists were celebrating.'

O'Hara had hardly blinked. 'So what happens to Sally, then?'

'OK – what about her?' There was a long, long silence. 'In a so-called *civilised* country like ours, should I be paying through the nose to get her the best treatment? Why should top treatment be a privilege for people like me with the dosh?'

'Oh, terrific! Same question – what are you going to do about it? Start the revolution?'

'Could do. Someone might have to. Anyhow, I've told you what I'm *not* doing – I'm not doing this any more. I'll find some other way. I'll try to make my own little bit of difference – write more radical lyrics, sing them round the clubs and colleges, go on a few marches, campaign like hell...'

'Hey-up, this sounds a bit political...' Nicky was coming over with the others, drawn in by the serious talk.

'...But most of all I'm going to give my own time to Sally. Sounds like she's had a bit of good news from Charlie; now it's going to be a few more cuddles from me.' He turned to the rest of them. 'God, does anyone remember cuddles?'

'Deano does – lucky man!'

'So I'm going to tour solo, or duo, or whatever, and strut my stuff around the country.'

'Boom-boom!' from Nick.

O'Hara's hands were folded across his chest. He was shaking his head. 'And what makes you think you're special?' he asked, quietly. He had to stop and clear his throat. 'You think that makes you different from the rest of us? That an Irish oik like me wouldn't have the sort of ideals Saint Stevie Peat has had revealed...?' He looked around at the others, but he seemed to know the answer.

'I'm just keeping away from my mum,' Paul Stoner said. 'But you can count me in on the cause.'

'There's not a crotchet of mine hasn't got a strong social conscience.' Deano carried on meticulously folding his frockcoat.

'So you see, we're all with you, bucko.'

And for the first time since Sally had been hurt at Sol Newman's, they saw Stevie fighting to keep the tears out of his eyes.

The police car taking Charlie back to Grove Road stopped short of the tape stretched along the pavement's edge. The road had been kept open but the Peats' block of flats was cordoned off. Two police officers stood outside the building while forensic officers in white protective clothing came and went. Already the press was there – a van with a dish parked on the forecourt of the garage opposite, and photographers up their stepladders on the pavement.

'You wait in the car, Charlie,' the WPC told him.

'I'll organise getting a pair of jeans out.' She opened the door. 'What room are they in?'

'Mine. Down the stairs, first left. But can't I choose them?'

'It's a crime scene. Forensics are crawling all over it. It's going to take some top persuading to get anything out at all…'

He blew out his cheeks. He'd had to make a fuss to come here in the first place. Imagine going to the Groans in a police car, wearing a T-shirt and jockey shorts! The street would die of shame. The police were sending someone there to take a full statement from him. And that was a downer because it was well at the bottom of his list of things to do.

The police driver sat fiddling with his sat-nav, entering the postcode of the Leytonstone house. 'What was the last letter again?'

' "R". "E, R. Six ER".'

'I'll try that.' Said as if the technology was right and it was this weird boy who'd got it wrong.

Charlie turned his head away from the long lenses and gave the media the back of his head. He'd had a quick wash at the police station, but he wasn't going to be photographed with make-up still smeared above his eyes and a red smudge around his mouth. He kept his eyes fixed on the Grove Road door. Part of him wanted to be inside it, and part of him didn't. Yes, it was his home – but it had been the place where he'd been frightened out of his life, and beaten up, and almost killed.

'Charlie!'

Maevy-baby was coming along to the car, half intercepted by a policeman, but allowed to pass because her flat was inside the cordon.

'It's all over the news. Lord, who would have imagined…?'

'Thanks for coming to complain about the boiler.'

'Needs fixing, that contraption.' She laughed. 'But where's your mother, Charlie? And please don't tell me Croydon.'

'It's a long story.' He got out of the car. No one stopped him. The driver looked round, but he wasn't bothered – there was a colleague on the pavement. 'I'll tell you later.' He smiled. 'I'll give you an exclusive.'

Reporters were calling from across the road.

'Charlie!'

'Mr Peat!'

'How do you feel?'

'Were you hurt?'

'Give us a wave, Charlie.'

'Would you do me a favour?' he asked Miss Portland.

'Someone's in there getting me a pair of jeans because I can't go in. Could I put them on and clean up a bit in your place?'

She looked at his smeary face and didn't hesitate. 'Of course you can. We're not having you dressing in the street. Even Grove Road has its behaviour code...'

The WPC came out of the flat with the jeans over her arm: not Charlie's first choice but they'd do. His dad would soon be home from Travonia, so he'd only be at the Groans' for a day or so.

'This is Miss Portland. She helped me escape from the flat,' he told the WPC.

'Ah. Very well done, ma'am.'

'Charlie's going to wash and change in my place,' Maevy-baby told her. 'He's not doing it in front of the world's press. Your car can wait five minutes?'

The WPC looked at the policeman on doorstep duties, who just flexed his neck muscles. It wasn't his decision.

'We'll have to be quick. A detective's on his way to Charlie's grandparents'.'

'He can wait five minutes.'

'She,' the WPC corrected her.

The three of them went into the next-door flat, the two women doing their best to shield him from the cameras. Her flat had the same layout as the Peats', the opposite way round: the front door opened onto the main living room, and a corridor led to the bathroom, the main bedroom and the stairs led down to the basement floor.

'I expect you know where the bathroom is?' Maevy-baby asked him. 'We'll wait for you in here.'

Charlie took his jeans from the WPC, and went along the corridor.

'Do sit down, young lady. Would you like to see the news? They say they've caught one of the suspects already.'

He closed the bathroom door. Quickly, he cleaned the remains of the make-up from his face. Now his eyes looked his own again, and he flashed them at himself in the mirror. He pulled on his jeans, tore off some lavatory paper to use for tissues and put them in his right hand pocket; and slipping his left hand into the other pocket, he posed for a second in front of the big mirror over the bath. He was alive! An hour ago he was going to be killed – in a terrible and painful way, he knew. He was breathing, he was looking at himself in a mirror, his eyes were open, he could wink at himself. And he had a very special friend called Francine, and a mate called Bijan, and a mother who was going to hear some good news –

which he was going to give her as soon as he could get away from the Groans, although that wouldn't be easy after the trick he'd pulled.

But, what was this in his left-hand pocket? He pulled it out. It was a very crumpled tenner, looking as if it had been through the washing machine. *Wash-dosh* – it sometimes happened, and it had happened today! His heart started beating to a quicker rhythm, his head felt lighter. Every hour, every minute, every second had counted from the beginning; ever since his mother had been admitted to Stage Left his life had been driven by visiting her with every bit of comfort he could conjure up: chocolates, jellies, blue irises, himself – and he had good news to tell her. And now with what he'd got in his pocket he could do it sooner rather than later...

Quietly, he opened the bathroom door – and to the sound of Maevy-baby's voice from the living room he crept down the stairs to the kitchen, slipped out through the back door, and ran across the patio to where he could climb over the wall. To head down Aberavon Road to Mile End tube, and out to Debden ...

The Groans and the police could wait, and for longer than him getting to Stage Left and back. They could start a manhunt – or he might phone to tell them he was OK – but he wasn't showing up at the Leytonstone house tonight until he'd done something else as well: after seeing his mum he'd use the rest of this dosh to take him to Blackwall College and the Friday-night rehearsal of Rubber Girders, where he couldn't wait to see the look on Francine's beautiful face.

ENCORE

*It was tenser than any concert gig, going out live to millions
– Sol Newman Presents on Sky Arts Live. All around the
studio, performers were set up in their own individual spaces,
with special guests sitting at blue bistro tables, Charlie, his
mother and Francine at one of them and a cluster of fans
standing behind. In the centre of the floor Sol Newman
walked from one spotlight to another to introduce a band,
to play along on clarinet or saxophone, or to accompany a
singer with his Sol Searching Band.*

*Charlie's heart started beating faster as Sol put down
his sax and spoke into the camera. 'And now, ladies and
gentlemen, the man and the band that survived the
Travonia terrorist campaign – touring Britain to full houses
of marvellous fans: I give you, Stevie Peat and No Rider!'*

*Coming in on the swell of the applause, Stevie counted
in the band. 'One, two, three, four' – and off they went with
their trade mark song 'Hold Back the Thames'.*

'Shut the river
Raise the boom
Send them back
We ain't got the room…'

– jumping the place through the number and finishing to whoops and cheers, and to Sol Newman coming over to sit at Sally's table. Charlie tried to swallow his nerves – but if his mother was feeling the tension, too, she wasn't showing it, which was a great sign. She was a bit fuller in the face these days, but she was still beautiful with her gleaming hair and soft make-up.

'And now to the lovely Sally Julien. Lovely to see you, and as gorgeous as ever.'

'Thank you, Sol.' Sally held her face steady.

'The wife of the talented Stevie Peat of No Rider, and someone we can't wait to book onto the show again.'

'Sometime,' said Sally, 'I'm not out of the woods yet... But I reckon I can see the light through the trees.'

'Come back, Sally!' someone shouted to a big whoop.

'Six months, a year,' Sally told Sol, 'perhaps with my old friend Ron Moreton...'

'Great pianist. Be wonderful – and well worth the wait.' Sol stood up. 'Sally Julien, ladies and gentlemen.' He walked back to the No Rider stage. 'And now a change of mood, the song no one got to hear back in May at the Dynamo Stadium, Travonia. The YouTube sensation that's taking thousands of internet hits.' He threw a wide, ringmaster's gesture, 'Stevie Peat, Deano Rivera, Sean O'Hara, Paul Stoner and Nicky Harris with "Street Dirt"!' He picked up

his clarinet to take up the melody line with them. Nicky hit the drums, and Stevie put his mouth to the mic.

'What do you do in the fight to survive
When you can't get the grub that you need?
Who's gonna help to keep you alive
When the fat cats keep feeding on greed?
Eh?
What do you do when the sky's falling down
And you're freezing with nowhere to go?
Who's got a shed, or a bed in the town
When you're losing your heat in the snow?
Eh?
We need community, human-kind, friends we
    never know,
Else, it's gold dust when you're on the up
But street dirt when you're low.'

Charlie sat there, trembling, and welling up. He was going to cry; this was his dad singing from the heart, the song he'd written that made him want to fight for a Stage Left for everyone who was ill. Charlie Peat was going to make a fool of himself on national TV. But as he closed his eyes to hold back the tears, Francine's hand quietly gripped his own, squeezed it, and she whispered, 'Great stuff! You can own up to being Stevie Peat's son – and I'm so proud of that.'

Sally reached across the table and stroked his arm. 'Chin up, Prince. Listen to your mum. Deep breaths, and think of all the music to come.'

And he just about managed to say: 'I'll come on here one day and sing Stevie's song.'

But Francine was shaking her head. 'Oh, no you won't. You'll come on here with me and Rubber Girders, and sing us one of your own…'

Can't get enough of Bernard Ashley's books?
Read on for an extract from
No Way to Go – available now!

Chapter One

Amber Long stared into the policeman's face. Her eye shadow and lip gloss made it very clear that she was giving Thames Reach Academy a miss that Friday, which wasn't a drama day with Mr Pewtrell. But they weren't sending the law round to the flats for skivers, were they?

'Mrs Long?' the policeman asked.

Amber snorted. 'Do I look like Mrs Long?' So what game was her stupid father playing in prison, getting her mum a knock-up at nine o'clock in the morning?

'Is Mrs Long in?'

'No, she isn't.' Amber stuck out her jaw. Her mother Debra – *Debs* to her boyfriends – hadn't been home for a couple of nights.

'Do you know where she is, love?'

'Do you know where Osama Bin Laden is?'

'And your father?'

'Ask the governor of Marwood prison.'

The policeman – young and pimply – was breathing deeply, and his face was going blotchy. From his looks this wasn't a cat-and-mouse game he was enjoying, the way some of them would draw things out when it was a half-dressed teenage girl they were talking to. 'I need to see your mother.'

'Well you can't. You'll have to come back.'

The PC looked both ways along the walkway. He glanced down at his radio, but taking another deep breath he came out with it. 'Have you got a younger brother? Connor?'

'He *can't* go to school. He got the boot. No one'll have him.'

'Can I come inside, Miss?'

'You going to get your truncheon out?'

But the young policeman was already taking off his helmet and sliding past her into the narrow passage. As soon as they were in the kitchen, he said, 'I'm afraid I've got bad news.'

'What's that?' But Amber knew the answer as soon as she asked. She was bright. It wouldn't be her father, and it wouldn't be her mother – he'd asked where they were. And when he'd mentioned her brother he'd said his name. It had to be Connor.

'Your brother . . . Connor Long . . . he's dead.' The policeman reached out a hand to her shoulder but didn't touch. 'He's fallen off a balcony over at Riverview House. Paramedics said he died on impact. He didn't suffer, love.'

And Amber crumpled, not onto a chair but down onto the floor. 'The silly little toe-rag!' she shouted into the tiles. 'Oh, the silly little fool!' But straight off she was kneeling up again. 'No – he couldn't!' she screamed at the policeman. 'He wouldn't! Not my Connor! He's too good a climber! He'd never fall off anything!'

'Connor! *Connor!* Who's done this? What've you been up to?' Along the pavement Amber Long pushed a PC aside, ducked under the tape, and ran to where an officer was photographing a chalked outline on the concrete. It looked like a cartoon of a kid asleep. '*Connor!*' she screamed, kneeling and pummelling the ground with her fists – raising her head to shriek '*No!*' at the tower block.

Sunil Dhillon, the trainee reporter, wrote *Connor* in his notebook.

The evidence officer cased his camera. 'Excuse me, miss . . .' He put a hand towards her.

'I'm his sister!'

'I'm very sorry.'

The PC who had been pushed aside was with them now, helping his colleague lift Amber gently to her feet, passing her over to a female officer. 'OK, OK, love, Susan'll take care of you.'

'Yeah – come on, sweetheart.' The officer led Amber to where a colleague poured a mug of coffee from a flask. 'Were you the only one at home?'

Sunil Dhillon leaned as close to the tape as he was allowed.

'Yeah.'

'And what's your name?'

'Amber. Amber Long.'

Sunil wrote *Long* in his notebook.

'Is your mother coming?'

'She's not there.'

'Where is she, Amber?'

'Out. Dunno.'

The inspector had come over and was nodding, followed by Dermot Mark who no longer had a camera available. 'I'm very sorry,' the inspector was saying. 'Tragic. Would you be prepared to come down to the station and give us some more details? Get away from here . . .'

Amber stared at him. Couldn't the man understand? 'I don't *want* to get away from here! Not yet. Then I want to see him.' Determined, no buts. She handed back her mug, pulled out her mobile phone, and tapped in eleven fast digits. Her mother changed phones the way she changed her knickers – but this just might get to her . . .

'Is that your mother you're calling?'

Amber snapped the phone shut. *Number not recognised.* She sat on the low wall, along from the reporters.

'Let me know when you're ready and you can go in a car with the detective constable there.' The inspector nodded towards a young man in a cheap suit.

Amber stared at him, through him. Who could she

trust? What did she dare say to anyone? Because she knew something they didn't. She knew something that opened up a whole different can of worms. *She knew without doubt that Connor had not slipped.* Her kid brother had been deliberately pushed, murdered. Some villain had killed him. When he was little, Connor had climbed before he walked – over the side of his cot, up into his high chair; and then as an infant up onto the garages at the back of the flats. From the off, being somewhere high was like a drug to Connor: the flat roof of the nursery, then the school, the community centre, the steep church; and there was nothing that gave him more of a laugh than some do-gooder turning out the fire brigade to save him; by which time he'd come down another way. He was king at it. Take him to Everest and he'd be up it like a shot – in flip-flops and a blindfold, if asked. So Riverview House with its window ledges and balconies and satellite dishes was a breeze to a climber like Connor. If he'd bothered with Riverview House that morning – and why in hell would he, with all the other new stuff being built around here? – he'd no more come off it than someone lying in bed would suddenly fall out for no reason. No. He'd been pushed, or thrown. There was murderous stuff going on! Amber's eyes were dry now, and clear.

'Sunil Dhillon, BBC TV,' Sunil started, from along the wall. 'I'm very sorr—'

'No – *I'm* sorry, sir!' the inspector interrupted, putting

himself between Amber and the trainee. 'You know the form.' And he organised the reeling out of more incident tape, and the shunting back of the media.

The young detective in the suit had walked over. 'I can understand you wanting to stay for a bit,' he said to Amber. 'Don't come before you're ready.'

Amber was caught on a sudden intake of breath. *Wanting to stay for a bit?* She shouldn't be here in the first place! She should be at the O_2 getting tickets for Half Past Yesterday! That was the real world. This was untrue! Crazy stuff! *Connor – DEAD?* What rubbish was that? What she wanted to be doing was cuddling him, and tickling him, and bouncing his bony body on the bed till the springs went, working him up to those shrieks and screams that always got their mum shouting. Connor Long was Amber's baby brother – he'd always been: he was special – not some chalk outline on the ground . . .

So, yes, she wanted to stay for a bit – where he'd died.

They found Debra Long: with a male friend, Winston, standing smoking outside A Cuppa Coffee in Lewisham High Street. At the police station Amber had come up with some names her mother sometimes mentioned – one of which rang a bell with the detective constable, who'd arrested the guy three months before. This led him to Winston's flat, where Winston's pregnant girlfriend pointed them in the direction of Lewisham.

At the first sight of the law coming towards them Debra and Winston shifted to go; but it could only be back into the coffee shop, so they faced it out.

'Debra Long?' the female officer asked.

'What?'

'Well, I'm very sorry, Debra – but I need a word. Do you want to come over to the car . . .?'

Winston looked at his watch. 'Gotta go, Debs. I'm serious late, babe.' And he went.

Debra trod on her cigarette and went with the officer and the young plain-clothes man, over to the police car at the kerb. The woman in uniform got into the back with her.

'It's Connor, isn't it? You've pulled him for putting in a car window or something.'

'I'm sorry to tell you –' a hand on her shoulder 'he's dead, Debra. He's had a fatal fall . . .'

'Oh.'

No shriek. No tears. No head slumped onto her chest or raised to heaven. Debra simply stared ahead. At which the DC in the front of the car switched on the ignition and drove them towards Thames Reach and the King George VI Hospital: where Amber and another female officer were waiting for them, round at the back in the mortuary area.

Amber saw her mother get out of the car, still wearing the straight black coat she'd put on to go out three days before. 'They told you? You know about Connor?'

'Yes.' Short, terse, dry-eyed as Debra hugged her daughter – but not for comfort, more like a handshake. 'You seen him?'

'Wouldn't let me, till you got here. Once they'd found you.'

'Yeah, well . . .' Debra turned to the young man in the suit. 'I'm here, aren't I?' She held her head erect, the modern haircut only slightly blown, leaving a strand across her left eye. She still looked young, considering the drink and stuff she did. Smelt a bit smoky, that was all.

'This way.' The DC's voice was low and soft, had been for everything he'd said to Amber. They went inside the mortuary where in the centre a small body on a trolley lay covered with a purple shroud. The mortuary attendant in his dark suit went to its head.

Amber found it hard to breathe. The air in there smelt of a mix of disinfectant and incense; but it wasn't that: it was the sickening fact that little Connor was dead. He would never again go out on one of his climbs, or sneak indoors with a pirate DVD, or bring her a vodka-kick, or bust his bed in a play fight. Amber couldn't even swallow – and she thought she might throw up. But somehow she held on – for Connor.

'Don't worry, love, he looks OK,' the attendant said quietly, reaching for the shroud and slowly drawing it back.

Oh God, wouldn't it be great if it was some other kid?

What if they'd made a mistake? If it could only be some other kid – just not her Connor!

But there lay Connor Long, ten years, three months, and two days old, cropped dark hair, eyes closed, looking the way Amber would see him some mornings when she rousted him out of his bed. Except this morning he'd woken early – and gone to sleep seventy years too bloody soon . . .

It was the holding of breath that could be heard. Until Debra spoke. 'Yes, that's him,' as if she were in some other reality. 'That *was* him.' And she turned away and walked out of the mortuary like a figure in a jerky film.

Amber stood staring at her brother as the shroud was replaced – and didn't feel the DC's comforting hand on her arm. Now she swallowed; and vowed to herself that Connor Long wasn't going to be in the past to her – the fact that he'd ever lived and been her brother was going to be the future. Because she knew right now, standing here, that she was never going to sleep peacefully again until she knew who had pushed this climbing boy who would never have slipped.

No Way to Go

'A tautly written,
tough-talking teenage
crime story...'
Jacqueline Wilson

Bernard Ashley

Amber is shocked when her
brother falls to his death from a
tower block. She's convinced it
wasn't an accident, and so begins
her journey to discover the truth
and bring some kind of justice for
Connor. With twists, turns and a
fabulous multi-layered plot,
Bernard Ashley has created a
thrilling and engrossing tale.
Set in south east London, this is
an incredibly gritty and
absorbing novel.

Also available
as an ebook

ORCHARD BOOKS
www.orchardbooks.co.uk